TEASED BY FIRE

MOLLY O'HARE

COPYRIGHT

Molly O'Hare
First Print: October 2018
Be You Publishing, LLC
www.MollyOHareauthor.com

ACKNOWLEDGMENTS

First, I want to thank YOU. Seriously, thank you!

I want to thank my husband, for always having my back. My friend, my editor, and one of my biggest supporters, Karen. KB: Love you guys.

Richelle – I can't believe a small conversation about a website theme started a beautiful friendship. You've been there through it all. The ups, the downs, everything. I cannot believe what an amazing friendship we have formed and in such a short time. I love you so freakin' much. You are the ultimate Great White shark, and you better never change.

Brittney, Julia, Ari – I think back at when I started this journey and love that you lovely ladies are right there. From the beginning, your support has meant so much to me. I would never be able to do it without you ladies. I love you all so much.

Christina – I am so thankful for you. You've helped me so much, you and J.E. have been so freaking amazing I don't even know how to thank you.

I also want to thank Angela Verdenius. I am so honored

to call you one of my good friends. You have been so unbelievably amazing in so many ways. I love you so much.

I do not really know how to thank any of you other than offering to give you my undying love, which you already have. No, take backs!

DEDICATION

I dedicate this story to you.
You are beautiful.
You are strong.
You are a freakin' unicorn.
I've said it before and I will continue to say it. You are perfect just the
way you are. If anyone tells you something different, mentally throat
punch them. (Please don't do it for real unless you want jail time. I
am not responsible for it. – Although, if they said jerk things to you,
they probably deserved it.)
This story goes out to all of you.
Be you.
Always.
Fuck everyone else.

CHAPTER ONE

OLIVE QUINN GLARED daggers at her traitorous best friend, Miranda Parker, as the bane of her existence moved yet another piece of his furniture into her apartment.

This was all Miranda's fault.

"Stop trying to murder me with your eyes, Olive." Miranda sighed in annoyance as she pushed the hair out of her face.

That only caused Olive to glare harder in her friend's direction. "I will not stop trying to murder you with my eyes," Olive whisper shouted. "It's your fault *he* is moving into *my* apartment."

"What the hell did you want me to do, Olive? I knew I couldn't leave you stranded to pay the rent on your own. You're just pissed I'm moving."

"Damn right, I'm pissed. If I were you I'd check every box you packed for surprises." Olive squinted her eyes harder in Miranda's direction trying to intimidate her.

Miranda shook her head. "How many times are we going to go through this? If I thought I had a chance of getting the job, I would have told you. I would have thought hell would've frozen over first."

"And yet here we are. Hell must be mighty cold right now."

"I'm sorry, okay. I'm freaking sorry."

At Miranda's defeated posture Olive softened. "No, I'm the one that's sorry. You've got your dream job now. I need to stop being angry and just be happy for you."

"It's a lot changing all at once."

Olive looked at Miranda, her eyes filling with tears. "I'm going to miss you. We've been stuck together since the first grade."

"Nothing's changing," Miranda tried reassuring her.

"Everything is changing. You're moving clear across the country and I only found out two days ago. I haven't had time to accept the fact my only friend is leaving me." Her eyes narrowed. "And, to top it all off, you went behind my back and gave your *brother* your room."

Miranda sighed before crossing her arms over her chest. "I don't understand why you are freaking out so much. Yeah, Hank is an ass, but if you both stay out of each other's way, you'll be fine. Plus, I've brought you the best research tool a romance writer could ever ask for. You'll be able to get up close and personal experience on how he operates. I brought you a gift."

"If you mean the gift of an STD infested manwhore? You can keep it." Olive's eyes widened as everything clicked into place. This wasn't her best friend. There was no way in hell her best friend who she'd known for years would actually be doing this. That settles it. She'd somehow been abducted by aliens and the person standing in front of her was an imposter. *This is it. This is the zombie apocalypse we've all been waiting for.* Olive quickly grabbed Miranda's arms examining them for any sign of an implant.

2

Miranda snatched her hands back. "Jesus, Olive, what are you doing?"

"Checking to see if you have a tracking device somewhere," she said as a matter of fact.

Miranda rolled her eyes. "Do you ever live anywhere other than your fantasy world?"

Offended, Olive crossed her arms over her chest. "Hey, my weird brain is a masterpiece. How else do you think I come up with my stories?"

"I don't know how you function when all you think about is the zombie apocalypse or some strange alien race invading the earth."

Olive pointed at her head. "This imagination makes me money."

"How? Your brain makes zero sense. You don't even write the shit that goes on in your mind." Miranda shook her head. "Olive, you write contemporary erotic romance. Please explain to me how a brain so involved in aliens and zombies writes hardcore romance with alpha males that make all women drool?"

Olive shrugged. "I don't know. I think it's a weird yin and yang thing, you know, balance to the Force and what not."

"Fuck!" They heard from the other room as a loud bang echoed throughout the space.

Olive's eyes narrowed back at her friend as her lips thinned. "He's a big oaf, and he's gonna use his big oaf muscles to make holes in my walls."

Miranda crossed her arms over her chest. "All right, Olive, I get it. You're fucking pissed. Okay. If I were you I'd be pissed too, but there is nothing we can do about it now. Hank is moving in. Right now, as we speak. He needed a place and you need someone that can pay half the rent. End. Of. Story."

Olive knew Miranda was right, but that didn't stop the betrayal and hurt from running through her. Within two days, everything she was accustomed to had been upended. That's a lot for anyone to take in.

"It's not like he'll be here often anyway," Miranda remarked. "He's always at the fire station, and when he's not, he'll be out with his flavor of the week."

"That isn't the point. With Hank the Tank…" Olive physically revolted. "I hate that nickname everyone calls him."

"It's stupid, I agree."

"Back to what I was saying," Olive started again after shaking the thoughts from her head. "With Hank moving in, I can't be me anymore. Olive Quinn: awkward, hates people, never goes outside or wears a bra. I'll be banished to my room or *forced* to wear a bra. I don't want to wear a bra. Bras suck and stifle my creativity. Oh God, don't even get me started on underwires. Who the hell came up with underwires for bras, anyway? I bet you it was a man. Yup, it had to have been a man. A woman wouldn't have invented something that after a little while, a hard metal wire pokes out and causes you excruciating pain; when all you want to do is walk to the store and buy some snacks. But no, instead I'm walking down the sidewalk discreetly trying to move the wire to a place where it's not trying to puncture through my skin and kill me."

Miranda chuckled. "You have a point about the bra, but you said the same thing about pants and you've grown accustomed to wearing them."

"*Not by choice!* I only wear them because you kept the air on "cold as fuck." If I didn't wear pants these thunder thighs would have gotten frostbitten."

"I keep it cold because you have that weird obsession with the holidays."

"I do not!"

Miranda's brow rose before she pointed to the corner of Olive's bedroom. "You have a freakin' Christmas tree up."

"Yeah, what's your point?"

4

"It's the middle of *June*. No one needs a Christmas tree up in the middle of June."

Olive held her hand to her chest as if she'd been shot. "How can you say that?"

Miranda instantly rolled her eyes. "It's the *middle of June*. That's how I can say that."

"Haven't you heard of Christmas in July? I'm just a few weeks early."

"Christmas in July," Miranda scoffed. "Olive, you haven't taken it down in the three years we've lived here."

"Damn, Scrooge much? Sorry, my joy of the holidays makes you a bitter humbug."

Miranda held Olive's shoulders. "Please leave this apartment more often and get some fresh air. I really am worried about you."

"Do not shit all over my love of the happiest time of the year. And, stop deflecting on the fact that *you* went behind my back and moved in your brother."

"Think of all the material for your books you'll get now." Miranda swiped her hand toward the bedroom door. "His friends are delicious, what more can you ask for? Hot firemen as your personal research subjects. You can save your computer from all the viruses from those porn sites you..." She made air quotes. "...use for research."

"Hey, don't knock it. Those sites are a golden tool for my line of work."

"Whatever. It's done. Now, let's go back out there and get the rest of my stuff packed away."

Olive huffed before following her friend. "Remember those *research subjects* include your brother the next time you read one of my books." Olive couldn't help the smirk that spread across her face when Miranda's eyes widened. *Take that you, traitorous devil woman!*

"Oh shit, what have I done?"

5

Olive pushed Miranda's shoulder shoving her toward the door. "Serves you right."

As they walked back into the living room, Olive's heart stopped as she saw a shirtless, sweaty Hank standing in the middle of the room. How in the hell was it possible to look *that* good? He had muscles for days. Her eyes went to his abs as she started mentally counting them. Sure, half the men in her books were described like him, but that was in her mind. Men did *not* look like them in real life. And, why the hell was he looking at her like she was a tall glass of water and he was a man dying of thirst?

Her whole body shivered. She one-hundred percent stepped into an alternate universe.

"There you two are," Hank remarked. "I thought you'd left all the work to us." He nodded his head toward his station buddies that'd agreed to help move Miranda out and him in.

Olive looked around at the men scattered throughout the room. It was like a *Hot Fireman/Paramedic* calendar threw up in her apartment. Maybe this wasn't such a bad idea after all.

She turned toward her friend and smirked, which made Miranda blanch for a brief second before she spoke. "No, we haven't left. We were just discussing something in Olive's room," Miranda announced before making her way to one of the many boxes in the living room.

"That so, and what did you and Olive Oil need to discuss?" Hank smirked in her direction.

"Do not call me that!" Olive glanced around the room for something to throw at his head. She'd grown up with Hank teasing her every chance he got, and if he thought she would just stand by and let him do it in her own home he had another thing coming.

At her annoyance, Hank chuckled. "Oh, I think living with you will be lots of fun, Olive Oil."

Olive turned back to Miranda ready to demand she make him leave when Hank yelled out, "Any of you seen Dog?"

A chorus of *no's* rang out throughout the room which made Olive roll her eyes. "Let me guess, another one of your degenerate friends?" she asked, glaring at Hank.

His eyes brightened with laughter as his smile grew wider. "Miranda didn't tell you about Dog?"

Olive's eyes shot to her best friend who now busied herself with removing an invisible piece of dirt from her shirt. "No, I guess that tidbit of information escaped her," Olive sneered.

Hank disappeared out of the room leaving Olive with her brow raised and her arms crossed at his sudden departure. *Well, okay then. Clearly living with Hank was not going to be a walk in the park.*

A few minutes later she heard Hank shout, "Found her!" He then made his way back into the living room. That's when Olive spotted the largest Maine Coon cat she'd ever seen in her life cradled in Hank's arms.

"What is that?"

Hank pat the cat on its head causing the ginormous thing to tilt its face in his direction seeking out more attention, or possibly meat from a small animal being used as a sacrifice. "This is Dog," he said with a grin.

That's when she snapped. "Who the fuck names a *cat* Dog?"

CHAPTER TWO

"Dude, Hank, she looked pissed," Hank's longtime best friend and fellow firefighter, Lucas said as he shoved another piece of pizza in his mouth.

"Yeah man, she looked pissed." His buddies all chimed in together as they sat around the table scarfing down their food.

Hank smirked. "Did she? I hadn't noticed." Olive *did* look pissed and he loved every second of it. The moment he brought Dog out, Olive's arms crossed under her chest pushing those delectable tits up to her chin. He'd chastised himself for fantasizing about those babies for years. Your younger sister's best friend was off-limits though. That's written in the man code rule book. However, when it came to Olive Quinn, there was something about her that made him forget his own name. One look at her and he wanted to break all the rules.

Hank remembered coming home from a summer away, working at his uncle's construction company, and seeing just how much Olive had grown into her body. It was the first time he took notice of her more than his little sister's best friend.

Lord have mercy!

And as Olive got older, she only filled out more and more. It was like she was made to purposely get his motor running. She had hips that begged to be held on to. Thighs that he knew would cushion him as he fucked her, and a stomach that would be soft against his head as he'd fall on top of her after a fuck session that would blow them both away.

Her curves made his mouth water. He wanted nothing more than to sink his teeth into her and get lost inside of her.

But, he couldn't.

And, he shouldn't. It didn't matter how many times she'd appear in his fantasies. No one should have those types of feelings toward their little sister's best friend.

Olive was meant to be worshiped from afar.

That was until everything changed.

The moment his sister announced she was leaving and Olive needed a roommate he jumped at the opportunity. Even if he wasn't in the market at looking for a new place to live he would have arranged it.

The chance to finally get up close and personal to his little wallflower made his skin heat. Hank was tired of denying himself and at thirty-four, why the fuck should he? He was tired of constantly sneaking glances at *his* Olive Oil. Especially, since the opportunities to get a glimpse of the elusive creature were few and far between.

He'd long since given up on seeing Olive in any social settings. Every time Miranda came out to the station, or to some party or event, Olive was never in tow. She stayed to herself with her head buried in a book or on her computer.

However, whenever he thought he'd figured her out, she'd never fail to do something to keep him on his toes.

Maybe that was one of the reasons he was so infatuated with her?

The day Olive surprised him by showing up to his fire-fighter graduation he almost shit himself. He'd never in a million years expected her to be there. But she was, and in all her glory too. Her chestnut hair was curled around the ends of her heart-shaped face. She wore a tight, almost second skin, sea blue dress that matched her eyes perfectly.

He was positive Miranda had forced her into that dress, *and* into coming to the graduation. The Olive he knew wouldn't be caught dead in something that revealing unless she was swindled by his all too persuasive little sister. That dress hugged every curve of her body.

He wouldn't have known, though. Olive had made a point to hide herself away under an oversized shawl. Hank only found out about his newfound Mecca when she tried to awkwardly hug him in congratulations. The moment his brain fully started to function he took his chance and pulled her body close to his. He remembered sneaking his right arm under her shawl and wrapping it around her. He did his best to mold her every curve to his body.

What's the use of hugging someone if you don't give it all you've got?

His dick hardened at the memory as he suppressed his groan.

His walk down memory lane was short-lived, though. He felt his fists clench at his side as he recalled she was on the arm of that asshole, Josh.

He never liked him.

There was something about Josh that was off. Hank knew his instincts were right when Miranda informed him that douchebag Josh had used Olive and then threw her away all while making her the laughing stock.

He had to stop his sister as she searched for places to hide a body. He didn't blame her, and if truth be told he was more than willing to take the matter into his own hands, but he knew Miranda being hauled away to prison would be worse on Olive than some asshole dumping her.

"Dude, you look like you are gonna fucking kill someone," Lucas said, drawing him from his memories.

"I'm just tired," he lied, while he contemplated looking up where Josh lived now and paying him a visit.

Lucas' brows shot to the ceiling. "You sure about that?"

"Yeah," Hank replied. Wanting to switch the conversation he also added, "Thanks for coming to help today."

"You know I'd help you no matter what."

"I know, that's what brothers are for." Hank pushed at Lucas' shoulder. Ever since they graduated from the academy, he and Lucas had bonded. They were also lucky enough to end up at the same station house once all was said and done.

He knew Lucas had his back, whether that be on the job, or in life.

"How do you think Olive's getting along with Dog?" Lucas asked.

A mischievous smile appeared on Hank's face. "Not sure, but if there was a problem Miranda would have text me by now."

"I hope you're right about that. When you announced we were leaving to get pizza she couldn't take her eyes off Dog. I honestly think you broke her. She didn't even acknowledge five guys leaving the apartment." Lucas' face broke into a ridiculously wide smile. "Dude, I think she might try and poison you."

"Good thing I've had medical training then."

"I'll be sure to remind you, you said that when we get the call you're incapacitated with foam spewing out of your mouth."

Hank threw his head back as he barked out a laugh.

"Ahh, he's fine. You probably won't see her anyway. She seems like the person to stay in her room and never come out," Rick, their chief medic at the station, chimed in.

That was about to change. The first second Hank got, he was going to drag Olive out with him. He could be very persuasive if he needed to be. What could he say? Persuasion runs in his family.

When Miranda informed him, living with Olive would be more like living on his own, he made her explain. According to her, Olive spent ninety-five percent of her time locked in her room doing God knows what. He didn't like the thought of that. The alpha male in him jumped at the thought of breaking her free.

There was adventure behind every door, and he damn well was going to show her.

He loved a challenge and Olive Quinn was the ultimate challenge.

Hank's mouth curved into a wicked smile.

Now that he lived with her, he was going to stop at nothing to make her his.

"That look on your face concerns me," Lucas remarked.

"This is just my face," he shot back as his smile grew even wider.

"That's what they all say before they do something stupid."

"I don't know what you're talking about." Hank laughed. Ignoring the commotion at the table as his friends started chatting about work, Hank started searching his pockets.

Fuck, not again! As his hands went in and out of his pants pockets he came up empty.

Lucas shook his head. "What have you lost now?"

Hank's eyes narrowed at his buddy. "What makes you think I lost something?"

"You've got that look again."

"What look?"

Tim shouted from the other end of the table. "The classic Hank the Tank look that tells all of us you've lost something."

"I am not that predictable." Hank's eyes narrowed.

"I got twenty on his keys," Tim said, one of the stations other medics.

"Twenty-five on his wallet," came from Rick.

"Fifty on his cell," Lucas announced.

"Fuck you, guys!"

"Nah, you're too bulky for me," Tim laughed out.

Hank shook his head ignoring their jabs as he searched for his phone.

How could you blame a guy for losing track of his shit when all he could wrap his head around was being able to see his fantasy girl every damn day?

A man's got priorities and right now, those involved Olive and figuring out ways to not only rile her up, but make her realize he's the one for her.

CHAPTER THREE

OLIVE STARED at the cat which now blocked her path from her bedroom to the kitchen. All she wanted was a glass of water, but no. She never thought she'd have to have a showdown in her own home.

She was already seething from Hank moving in, *then* finding out about this human child sized cat, but then the bastard announced he was going out for pizza.

Did he offer to bring her pizza back? No. See, *Bas-tard!* And then he left his cat just sitting here in the living room.

One more check mark in the Hank living here will be hell on earth column. *Where is the zombie apocalypse when you needed it?*

To top off her frustrations, Miranda, the sleuthing jerk of a best friend, hightailed it out of the apartment with her last box leaving Olive alone... with the cat.

The cat that was the size of a small child.

The cat that was staring her down, and she could swear it just licked its lips.

Olive quickly surveyed the room around her. She was

trapped. And by the looks of it, the cat was hungry, and Olive was on the menu.

"Nice kitty, you're so nice." Olive took a step closer to the cat, causing the creature to open her mouth and let out a hiss. "Oh, shit." Olive jumped back.

Let's try this again. "Hello, kitty. I only want to pass you to get into the kitchen. Is that okay? You're a very pretty kitty. You've got big dark eyes that are looking directly into my soul. And, you must take such good care of your teeth. They are so big and sharp. I know because you keep showing them to me. "

The cat meowed at her.

"Oh, right!" Olive hit the palm of her hand against her forehead. "You probably don't understand me. Should I meow at you? Would that be offensive?" Olive debated with herself.

Shaking her head, she did her best to come up with a game plan. *Okay, if you move fast, you can jump over the coffee table and then leap over the back of the couch. The cat won't know what hit her.* Making sure not to lose eye contact with the creature in fear of it figuring out her plan. Olive took a step to the left.

That's when *Dog* stood, eyeing her.

It was a standoff.

Both parties held their ground for about thirty seconds. The moment Dog made a step in her direction Olive took off running into the nearby joint bathroom.

She held her hand to her chest. "It's fine. Everything is fine. I can live off water from the sink." Quickly, Olive locked the bathroom door, just in case the creature knew how to work a handle.

She placed her hand back on her chest as she did her best to get her heart rate under control. Moving to the sink, she cupped her hands together and brought some water to her mouth. "Not ideal, but I can live with it."

Once her thirst was quenched, she looked toward the

bathroom door. As she decided to take a chance and run for it, she saw the shadow of an ominous figure pass in front of the bottom of the door.

"Oh God, it's waiting for me!" she shrieked. She watched as the shadow continued to move back and forth. Dog was the predator and Olive was the prey.

Well, that settled it. Placing her index finger on her chin she thought of ways she could rearrange the bathroom to make her new living arrangements more suitable. *The towels would be perfect blankets and pillows...* As she looked around and tried to decide what else she could do, she suddenly heard the front door open.

"Hank, is that you?"

She heard shuffling and then footsteps that stopped right in front of the bathroom door. "Miranda? Hank?" she called through the door again.

"It's me, Olive," Hank announced. "Are you okay?" The concern she heard in his voice made her brows knit.

No, she was not okay.

Her best friend abandoned her and dropped off her brother in her place. And, there was a supposed cat- the jury was still out on the actual species of the thing- that was trying to kill her. No, she was certainly *not* okay.

"Olive, are you in there?"

"Yes, I'm in here," she spat. "I'm trapped. Your stupid child cat bullied me."

She heard him laugh. "Dog is not a bully. Sure, she's a little intimidating, but not a bully."

"The hell she isn't!"

"She's tough. What do you expect a cat to be when she grows up at the station? She's got her wits about her and takes charge."

"She ran me into the bathroom!"

Olive heard Hank jiggle the handle. "Why is the door locked?"

"Because your monster cat probably knows how to open doors."

"Olive unlock the door."

"Not until it's safe."

"It is safe."

"Not while that *thing* is still out there lurking."

Olive heard more shuffling and a quiet 'for fuck's sake.' "There. I've got Dog in my arms. You can come out now."

Not sure if she believed him or not, Olive carefully unlocked the door. Opening it only a hair she saw the *creature* in Hank's arms along with a box of pizza on the coffee table.

New game plan. Run as fast as you can to grab the box of pizza and then to the bedroom. As she flung open the door, she realized her mistake. Pizza should not have come first. *Abort! Abort!*

Ignoring the tantalizing smell, she ran toward her room.

"No, you don't." Hank was on her faster than she could comprehend. Before she knew it, her legs were flying through the air, then she was placed upright on the couch. Hank standing directly in front of her.

"How in the hell did you do that?" She did her best to straighten herself.

"Practice." He smirked, which made her eyes narrow. "Didn't your mother teach you it's not nice to pick up people and throw them around?"

"I didn't throw you. I placed you gently." The joy in his eyes made her want to punch him.

"You probably pulled out your back."

"Are you saying I'm weak?" He had the gall to look hurt.

Olive could feel the gray hairs already forming on her head. "No, I'm saying you're an idiot." At her words, she heard the creature hiss from somewhere in the room. "Ahhh." Olive pulled her legs up.

"The cat isn't a shark, Olive Oil. Your legs hanging off the side of the furniture is not an open invitation."

"It tried to eat me."

"No, she didn't."

"Yes, it did!" She saw enjoyment in Hank's eyes which made her annoyance rise to an all-time high.

Hank must have realized her frustration because he held up his hands in surrender. "Okay, I give. The cat was trying to kill you."

"It was!"

"I believe you."

"And who in the hell names a cat, *Dog?*"

Hank sat on the couch next to her. "I do." He laughed, before opening the box of pizza and pushing it toward her.

Olive observed him carefully. *What was he playing at?*

"I found Dog when she was only a few weeks old," he said, picking up a piece of cheese pizza before handing it to Olive. "We were called to an abandoned warehouse that had gone up in flames. When the fire was finally out, I found her on top of her siblings and mother." A sorrowful look ran across his face. "She was the only survivor."

He reached down between his legs and plucked Dog into his arms. "The whole way to the station I kept an oxygen mask on her. She pulled through like a trooper. And for the next few weeks, me and the guys took shifts feeding her and making sure she would survive."

He scratched under her chin causing the monster to plop onto her back and submit to his ways. Which only annoyed Olive more, even cats were putty in his hands.

"She became our station's mascot." He looked at her, with joy in his eyes. "Most fire stations have dogs. We had a cat."

"So, you named it Dog?"

"I named *her* Dog."

"Why is she here and not at the station?" Olive asked while she shoved pizza in her mouth, eyeing the creature cautiously.

"About a year ago, we had a recruit join the house. One of our daily chores was to brush and take care of this gal." He scratched Dog under the chin. "It turned out the recruit was severely allergic, and with Dog's long hair the recruit had allergy attacks all the time. We realized it wasn't fair to Dog, or the guy to keep her there, so I took her home."

"And now she lives here. In my apartment. With you."

Hank smirked. "Yep."

CHAPTER FOUR

OLIVE TOOK a deep breath as she opened her bedroom door and peeked around the corner. She wasn't sure what form of hell she was about to walk into, but she knew something was coming, it always was.

Two weeks.

It'd been a total of two weeks since Hank moved in and every day had been worse than the day before.

"Don't worry, Olive. Hank will never be here." Olive's eyes narrowed at Miranda's lies.

The bastard was there *all the damn time*. Olive was also seventy-five percent sure Hank didn't know what a shirt was.

He never seemed to be clothed.

Never.

She wasn't one to complain about the view, but it was a distraction. Especially after his workouts. She could count the sweat droplets as they fell down his body.

His presence always surrounded her apartment. No matter how hard she tried, she couldn't escape him.

Scanning the room again, she saw no sign of him. Thank

God. Sure, Olive wouldn't deny he was good material for her books, largely since he refused to wear clothes.

But, that's all it was.

A half-naked fireman walking around her apartment.

Hank hadn't brought anyone home. Which part of her was thankful for. Seriously, who wanted to listen to two people going at it in the next room?

Especially Hank. *Eww!* She cringed.

However, the research part of her, the part that sought out any and all material she could use for her books, was pissed. Why wasn't this so-called Casanova laying on the moves to unsuspecting bar bunnies? Didn't he understand she had books to write? Characters to create? Her eyes narrowed. It was the only good thing about him moving in, and he was denying her his prowess.

Wait a minute? Her mind quickly changed gears. *Wouldn't bar bunnies be there just for that?* Olive bit her lip thinking as she pondered a potential research spot. *I could go to the bar down the street and observe the behavior of the* chase.

Quickly she banished that thought as she shook her head. "Nahh." No need to go out and interact with people, that's what the internet was for.

She wiped her brow. Human interaction averted.

Doing another scan of the apartment from her doorway, everything seemed to be in order.

Seemed was the keyword. Hank's constant need to get a rise out of her was taking its toll.

On day two of their new living arrangement adventure, Hank thought it would be knee-slapping funny to relabel all her ingredients in the kitchen. It only took one sip and the roar of laughter from Hank for her to realize she'd poured an unhealthy amount of salt into her coffee instead of sugar.

A smile grew across her lips. She'd won that battle,

though. After realizing what he'd done, she promptly walked over to him dumping the liquid on his head.

Luckily for him, it had cooled enough.

The bastard only laughed harder as he walked into the bathroom to shower.

Then, there was the time she found her hidden stash of Oreo cookies tampered with. No one wants to bite into their favorite cookie only to be assaulted with mint freaking toothpaste.

Nothing was safe anymore. And it was all Hank's fault.

Olive was over going into the living room to see the furniture rearranged, or the human-sized cat eyeing her like she was its next meal.

Going outside of her room was a war zone.

She was all for the zombie apocalypse, but not like this.

Taking a step into the living room, she glanced around. Everything *looked* normal. The furniture was in its rightful place and the creature was nowhere to be found.

Taking a quick peek toward Hank's room she noticed the door open, but there was no movement inside.

"Thank God." She breathed out a sigh of relief. Maybe he'd gone into work already?

Confidently, Olive walked to the kitchen with the plan of grabbing some snacks to hold her over for a while, as she entered her next marathon writing session. As she reached the pantry door in search of her goodies, she heard a grunt come from the bathroom. "Eep." She held her hand over her heart. Realizing Hank was indeed still in the apartment her panic started to rise. *Must work faster.*

She quickly grabbed some food and made her way back through the living room.

That's when she saw it.

Her goodies completely forgotten, fell from her hands

cascading onto the floor, as her mouth opened in utter shock and disbelief.

"He *fucking* didn't!"

Every book on her bookshelf was out of place. Some were upside down, others were on the floor, *nothing* was where it belonged.

Her chest tightened.

Her most sacred possessions had been tampered with. Moving back in disbelief her eyes hardened as her body tensed. "I'll fucking kill him!"

She ran to the bathroom and started pounding on the door. "Let me in, you asshole. So I can strangle you!"

Taking a step back she readied herself to fling her body full force into the door. *Excess body weight, don't fail me now!* Using all her strength, she leaped, her shoulder at the ready. However, her body never came in contact with the door. Before she knew it, she was flying through the air.

"Fuck, Olive." She heard a voice grumble as she felt her body collide with a wall of muscles. "Are you okay?"

Ignoring the fact her body was plastered against his wet chest, she jumped from his grip. "Am I okay? Am. I. Okay?"

"That's what I asked?" Hank had the nerve to fuckin' smile at her.

Kill him! She opened her mouth to tell him what for, when Hank moved his hands to his waist. That's when she realized he was only wearing a towel.

Not just any towel, though. Her *favorite* fluffy towel. She clenched her teeth as her breathing hardened. She was about to add his use of her towel to her list of grievances when he untucked the material around his waist and opened it slightly to readjust.

It gave her the perfect glimpse of his muscular thigh. The edge of the towel was only millimeters from giving her a show she'd never forget. Her mouth dried as heat poured low in her belly.

"Olive?" His voice held amusement.

Olive's eyes snapped to his. The gleam in his eyes had her cheeks heating.

Holy crapolie. Caught. Eww! Olive's face cringed. *You've been caught staring at Hank. Hank the Tank of all people!*

"What's got your panties in a bunch, Olive Oil?" He chuckled.

With those two words her anger came back full force, her lust thrown away. Taking a step closer to him she pushed her finger into his slick chest. "You've gone too far this time, Hank Parker."

His smile widened. "Whatever do you mean, little Olive Oil?"

Her arms crossed over her chest. She could feel her blood pressure rise. *Great, with my luck, I'll be on the floor having heart palpitations at any moment.* "The hell you do," she sneered.

Olive stomped out of the bathroom, leaving Hank to follow. When she made it into the living room she pointed to her bookshelf. "Fix it," she demanded. "Now!"

Hank leaned his shoulder against the doorframe of the bathroom crossing his arms over his chest, as he shot her a smug grin. "No."

Olive's eyes widened as she blinked a few times. "What do you mean no?"

"Exactly that." He shrugged. "No."

Her anger rose to an all-time high. *What the hell did he say? Fuck this!* The possibilities of her next move started raging through her head. *Take him down!* He had a lot of muscle on him, but if she timed it right she could do it. As the reality of the situation had her seeing red, she threw caution to the wind. She took her first steps like she was a prized stallion ready to win her next trophy. She screamed out a war cry as she took off running through the room.

That's when she heard the hiss of death come from the beast cat, toward her right. She was thrown off balance scanning for the cat to make its move and finally end her. "Shit!" she screamed as she lost her footing and fell backward onto the couch. Quickly she picked her feet off the floor shielding her legs from the attack she knew was coming.

Hank placed his hand on his stomach as he barked out a laugh at the show. "Damn Olive, who knew living with you would be so entertaining?"

She was about to scold him when the sight of *the beast* caught her eye. She pulled her body into itself. "There it is!"

That only made Hank laugh harder, as he walked into the room. "She only picks on you because you let her."

Olive's brow rose. "I let her?"

"Yeah, she thinks you're an easy target." He moved through the room.

Olive's face hardened. "Is that why you think you can pick on me? I *let* you." She huffed. "What a crock of shit that is."

Hank had the audacity to look wounded. "I don't pick on you."

Holy hell, Batman. This man was utterly insane. She pointed to her bookshelf. "What do you call that?"

"Oh," Hank remarked. "That's nothing, but pranks between roommates."

Her lips thinned as every muscle in her body tensed. "Pranks. Between. *Roommates*." The words ground out of her mouth. "No. I don't call that *pranks between roommates,* I call that torture." Her eyes broke from his as she looked back at her precious bookshelf. The shelf that held all her favorite books. The books she found her escape in. The books that changed her life.

She couldn't take this anymore.

She was tired of living in fear in her own home. Her shoulders fell as her vision blurred. "Why won't you just leave me alone?" Her voice broke.

Hank stared at her, his face calm, but his eyes held a pained look she'd never seen. He shook his head. "Fuck, Olive. I didn't mean to upset you." He walked closer, his movements jerky. "I was only joking around."

Moving further into the couch away from him, she shook her head as her voice cracked. "Not with my things. My babies."

Hank paled.

She wished she could find comfort in his rare behavior, but she couldn't. She had nothing left to give.

Olive was surprised when Hank crouched in front of her on the couch putting a stray piece of her messy chestnut hair behind her ear. "I'm sorry, Olive."

The sincerity in his eyes had her examining his features for the lie.

He spoke softly as he continued, "Let me put on some shorts and we can sort out your bookshelf. Okay?"

Hank had finally broken her. As she fought to control herself, her body took over. She looked into his eyes, and all she could manage was a small nod.

Hank cursed himself as he made it into his room. What the fuck was wrong with him? All he wanted to do was rile her up a bit. Not make her cry.

His fists clenched at his sides, as he did his best not to punch a hole in the wall. *What the hell was I thinking?* All he wanted to accomplish was keeping her on her toes. You know, to bring a little fun in her life, make her not take things so seriously.

He'd never known someone who would stay in their bedroom twenty-three hours of the day, doing God knows what. It wasn't healthy. He tried justifying his actions, but was coming up short. He'd be lying if he didn't admit to enjoying seeing the fire in her eyes when he got under her skin. The look she'd give him, would set him on fire. Who knew his wallflower had so much passion inside of her. He was dying to break her free. Force her to feel the flames inside of her.

Looking over his shoulder he saw her utterly defeated on the couch. "Fuck," he swore as he dug his fingers into the palm of his hand.

Taking a deep breath, he vowed to make this right.

He threw on some shorts as he noticed Dog had followed him into his bedroom. "You and I have got to make a pact, girl." He moved to the cat scratching her on the head briefly. "We both need to stop messing with Olive. Deal?"

The cat blinked slowly at him, before bringing her paw to her mouth to lick it.

"Really?" Hank stared at Dog. "We can play it your way. If you insist. No more cat treats unless you start being nicer." The cat stopped licking her paw and stared at him. "I mean it."

Dog plopped onto her back, showing Hank her belly. He laughed before moving to her. Scratching her briefly, he smiled. "Your charms will not sway my mission." Ignoring the cat, he took a calming breath before making his way toward the door.

When he stepped into the living room he saw Olive on the floor removing all her books from the bookshelves. Her shoulders dropped low as she rearranged them. Her defeated posture was like a punch to his gut. "Your books mean a lot to you, don't they?" he asked while he crouched down next to her. When she turned her doe eyes toward him, it was

27

another sucker punch to the gut almost knocking him on his ass.

"They mean the world to me," she whispered. Turning away from him, she went back to removing the books.

He'd never seen her like this. Reaching his hand on one of the books he brought it to the floor. "Let's get them back in order then."

For the next forty-five minutes they rearranged the shelves. He listened as she talked about each book.

Olive also made a new pile on the coffee table of books she wanted to move into her bedroom for rereading. He didn't quite understand why she needed to reread a book, you already knew what was going to happen so why bother, but her excitement on finding her hidden gems amongst the books excited him.

Her smile would spread from ear to ear as she exclaimed her love of this author or that book. She'd go on and on about plot twists and forgotten love. His heart melted the first time he saw her bring a book to her chest giving it a slight hug before placing it in its rightful pile.

This was Olive in her element and he loved every second of it. The wonderment in her eyes as she recalled her stories warmed him.

She was beautiful. He wanted to see this Olive more often. He needed to see it.

He was done with her hiding herself away in her room. As he watched her open another book and skim through a few of the pages, her smile widened across her face, he knew at that moment he'd do anything to see this every day.

"How about a truce?" he asked, distracting her from the book in her lap.

"Huh?"

He chuckled at her scrunched nose. "A truce. I promise to no longer mess with your stuff," he said matter of fact.

"Okay." She side-eyed him. "That's not a truce. That's just you saying you'll stop."

He held up his hands in surrender. "I will stop if you come out of your room more. I feel like my moving in here has banished you into your room."

"It has."

At least she's honest. "I want to change that. From today going forward, I promise no more pranks if you promise to come out of your room every once in a while. I prefer having a roommate I actually see from time to time."

"Why?"

"Because I like human interaction." He leaned back on his arms as the corners of his mouth rose into a smile.

"I avoid it at all costs." She moved from her sitting position and over to the coffee table.

"I've noticed." Hank stared at her as she worked on gathering her reread pile. He jumped to his feet moving to her side. "Here let me help you.

"I've got it."

"Olive didn't we just agree to be friends?" he smugly said before lightly pushing her out of the way.

He did his best not to laugh when her face scrunched. "I guess."

"Then let me help you." Ignoring her protest Hank walked into her room, with the pile of books in his arms, but he stopped frozen in his tracks. "Why the hell do you have a Christmas tree in your room?"

CHAPTER FIVE

THINGS HAD CALMED down around the apartment since Hank and Olive had their heart to heart. Although Olive was still forced to wear a bra, she did find herself relaxing and venturing out of her room more often.

Well, that was as long as the creature was nowhere to be found.

She also noticed Hank going out of his way to be nice to her. Sure, there were still times she found him purposely rearranging items in the apartment to get a rise out of her, but that was Hank. She'd come to expect it. Just as long as he never went near her books again. What was really surprising was how he'd even gone as far as picking up the groceries for the apartment, or doing any laundry he found.

This *was not* the Hank she knew. He was actually pretty in tune to her needs, even bringing her water from time to time.

Of course, at first, she suspected he'd poisoned it, but after making him drink the whole thing she realized he really was being nice.

Her eyes widened. *How long does it take for someone to assimilate into their surroundings?* Could Hank be some weird alien clone sent to destroy the world? What if he was slowly gathering information on her and waiting until her guard was down to make his move? *Oh shit, what if he has some weird alien device that he'll use to change me into a zombie.* Her heart rate increased. *What if I become the first zombie?* Quickly she searched her arms and body for anything out of the norm.

Realizing her insanity, she shook her head to get rid of the thoughts. She grabbed her laptop which was sitting on the coffee table in front of her and rearranged herself on the couch. She had a deadline to meet and thinking about Hank and his strange behavior was not going to get it done.

Actually, she pondered for a second. *I am working on describing a character. Maybe I can use some inspiration.* She noticed Hank's bedroom door was open. She started to lean over, trying to catch a glimpse of him. Straining her neck, she thought she could see some of his naked chest. Just a little farther...

That's when Hank walked out of his room and smiled her way.

"Ahh!" Olive fell to the floor, as she tried, and failed to right herself. Embarrassed, she made a show of looking for a nonexistent pen that had fallen on the floor.

"What are you doing, Olive?"

"Nothing," she said, blowing her hair out of her eyes once she finally pushed herself into a human position and not a catastrophic mess on the floor.

"You make a habit of crawling around on the floor, there sweet cheeks?" he teased.

Her face heated before she jumped to her feet. Thankfully her laptop hadn't hit the floor, so she grabbed it in one hand before sitting on the couch and putting it on her lap. "If you call me sweet cheeks one more time I will poison your coffee."

"That's your first mistake." He laughed. "Never show your

31

hand." He walked toward the couch plopping next to her. "Whatcha working on?"

"Work stuff."

He leaned over pushing his body weight onto hers. "And what's that?"

She quickly shut down her laptop. "It's boring." She moved her computer back to the coffee table before sitting back in her seat. "Don't you work today?" she asked, looking around the room. *Might as well deflect the best you can, Olive.*

Hank scrutinized her, she wasn't dumb. She could tell he was trying to figure out her lie. "Yes," he answered. "I go in at one."

Grabbing her phone, she placed it in front of his face. "It's already eleven thirty. You'll need to get ready soon. I know how you like to manscape."

Hank's brows shot to the ceiling. "Do you now?"

She blinked. "No, I mean, well, I assume you do. Don't most men like you do that kind of shit?"

He openly stared at her as his brow raised the impossible bit more. "Men like me?"

Her eyes widened. *Crap on a stick. Abort. Abort. Abort.*

Hank threw his head back as he barked out a laugh. "Olive Oil, you never cease to amaze me." Using his arms to push himself off the couch, Olive watched as his muscles rippled. How was it possible to look that good just getting up from the couch? As she watched his naked back move out of view as he walked toward his bedroom, his words registered. "Didn't I tell you to stop calling me Olive Oil?"

He turned facing her before giving her a wink. "Men like me don't listen."

Grabbing the napkin she'd used with her breakfast she wadded it up throwing it at his back. "Asshole."

Hank burst out laughing as he went into his room.

Fucker.

Ignoring him, she grabbed her laptop once again. Her deadline was calling. As she opened her writing program, she started scanning her recent work.

She'd somehow forgotten what she'd written this morning. Olive felt her skin heat as she read back through her last few paragraphs. She was knee deep in the beginnings of a sex scene where her alpha male had his plaything over his lap as he had his fingers deep inside her.

Instantly her mind started forming pictures of Hank having her bent over his lap, his fingers seeking out her- *No! Stop that! Right now.* She shivered. No way in hell was she going down that path. Shaking her head, she stretched her neck, before closing her eyes.

Get into your headspace, Olive. Ignore the sexy firefighter in the next room. She blanched.

What is wrong with you, Olive? It is not okay to have those types of thoughts about your best friend's brother. No, no siree bub. Not okay! Ignore the half-naked firefighter only a few feet from you.

Taking a deep breath, she did her best to ignore the humming coming from Hank's room as he moved around getting ready for his shift.

"You can do this," she whispered to herself.

Focus.

As she placed her fingers on the keyboard, the rest of the world melted away as she went into her writer's space. This is how it always happened for her. One moment she was questioning all her choices or being distracted by her surroundings and the next she was in the zone.

This was her happy place.

Hank made his way out of his bedroom searching everywhere. Once again, he couldn't find his keys to save his life.

Right now, he had about fifteen minutes to get out of the apartment and make his way to the station or he'd be late.

He wasn't going to let that happen. *Again*.

Hank knew the second he walked in late the guys would start to hound him and make bets about what he'd lost.

Rolling his eyes, his face hardened. Fuck them, he was not giving them any ammo.

Moving his search into the living room he noticed Olive's stuff was laid out on the coffee table. A smile spread across his face.

He couldn't help but enjoy the fact Olive had made more of an effort to come out of her room. Sure, he pulled back on his pranks. Kind of. He smirked. It was in his nature to tease her, always had been and always would. However, he made sure to stay clear of her books. He learned his lesson the first time.

The image of her broken on the couch still haunted him.

He scanned the room for her but came up empty.

He was however a little surprised she'd left her computer out in the open. That was the one thing he still questioned about her. Even though she came out of her room more, it was still like living with a ghost.

She'd either have her head in a book, or she'd be on her computer.

He'd even tried to have conversations with her, but whatever she was doing had her so engrossed, he was sure a bomb going off wouldn't tear her away.

Hank scratched his chin. After weeks, his curiosity was starting to get the better of him.

What was she always doing on her computer?

When he'd ask her, he'd get the brush off every time.

However... Hank looked around the room again.

No Olive.

A quick glance at his watch told him he was down to eight minutes. *Shit!* Should he risk it?

He heard a bottle fall in the bathroom. *That explains where she is.*

Hank did another glance around the room, in his gut knowing what he was about to do was wrong.

Fuck it. He moved the laptop, his lost keys totally forgotten. Right now, he was on a mission to see just exactly what his little wallflower had been up to.

Hitting one of the keys the computer roared to life causing his brows to raise as soon as the desktop showed. *Why wouldn't she have a password on here?* he questioned. Ignoring his instinct to inform her about cybersecurity, he opened her program that had recently been minimized.

Chapter Eight - Sky watched as Darren moved across the room toward her, a determination in his eyes she had never seen before.

"Repeat what you just said, Sky." His voice was dark and possessive. Heat poured into her core. She wouldn't let him see how he affected her though. He wouldn't win this time.

"Don't make me ask you again, Sky. Repeat what you said."

Squaring her shoulders Sky took a breath. Crossing her arms over her chest she spoke, "Make me."

Darren was in front of her in seconds. "Don't push me, Sky."

Jutting her chin out, she looked him in the eyes. "Make. Me."

Darren slammed his lips onto hers. His possession started to over take her as he cupped her cheeks in his hand. "Open," he demanded. When she didn't he bit her bottom lip. The sensation had her gasping for air while he took full advantage to plunder her mouth.

Every nerve ending in his body was on fire.

He pushed her back until her body landed against the nearby wall. Her legs instantly wrapped around his waist, where he ground his dick into her core.

"Harder," she pleaded, her hands tearing at his clothes. "Make me yours, Darren."

"You've always been mine, you stubborn woman. And, I'm about to remind you."

Hank's eyes widened as he skimmed the rest of the page. *Holy fucking shit!* He looked down at his hand, who'd gotten a mind of its own as it cupped his dick.

Jerking his hand away, he did his best to make sense of what he'd discovered.

Minimizing the program, he saw a folder on the desktop titled, "Published Books," opening it, he found it full of documents.

Holy. Fucking. Shit.

He moved his eyes to the bathroom door.

Everything finally clicked into place as he looked down at the folder once again.

CHAPTER SIX

HANK LAID on his cot in the station as his mind tried to process the information he'd found. In all the years he'd known Olive Quinn he'd never pictured her as an erotic romance author. Hell would have frozen over first. Who knew his anti-social, refused to show any hint of skin, Olive would make a career out of writing books about fucking?

Olive Oil had two sides. The side she showed everyone, and the one she kept hidden away.

Lust flared inside of him. He wanted to explore this other side of Olive. The forbidden side.

Fuck he wanted to explore *every* side of her.

Holy shit.

The moment he walked into the station house, he searched her author name on his phone. So far, he'd discovered fifteen books, a website, and all of her social media handles.

How had she been able to hide this all so well? No matter how many times he tried to grasp at the knowledge he'd found, he'd end up dumbfounded all over again.

A smirk spread across Hank's face. His double agent had some explaining to do. And, he was damn well looking forward to it.

He started exploring through her social media links. When he saw the number of followers she had, his mouth nearly hit the floor.

His little Olive Oil had herself a following. He couldn't help the smile that spread across his face as his heart swelled with pride.

As he scanned through her news feed, he found a plethora of posts. Some included new books and some random pictures with quotes on them. If he were being honest, he was one-hundred percent surprised at what he saw. Who knew one crash course in woman's romance would have his mind opening up to a world he knew nothing about.

Hank let his eyes scan further down the feed until a picture with flames caught his eye. There in front of him was a man dressed in his turnout gear minus the jacket. Actually, he had no shirt on at all, only his bunker pants with suspenders, with the guy flexing his abs.

Didn't this schmuck know how ridiculous he looked? Who the fuck dressed in their gear like that? *Idiot.*

Hank rolled his eyes as he continued his perusal of the photo. There was also a woman on her knees in front of the idiot firefighter, her naked back the only thing in view. The words, *"Who said fire play was dangerous?"*

"Fire *is* dangerous and no one should *play* with it," he scoffed, before he clicked on the link taking him to an eBook store. Once on the page he started to read the synopsis. When he finally realized what this story was truly about, his mouth curved into a smile. "A firefighter story... interesting." *Very interesting.*

Hank felt his body involuntarily move closer to his phone as he moved from the blurb to the reviews.

Five scorching hot stars! Was the first one he came across, followed by, *Quinn Sparks has done it again! Who knew a fireman's hose could be used so many different ways?*

Hank chuckled, if Olive wanted to know just how many ways a *fireman's* hose could be used, he'd gladly enlighten her. Skimming through the rest of the reviews, he saw the same things. *She's my favorite author.... I loved this book...* and so on and so forth.

He scratched his chin as he contemplated her use of a firefighter story. Maybe, just maybe, there was a chance for him yet.

"First you come in late and now you're lazing around fucking off on your phone?" Lucas bellowed as he made his way into the room.

Hank pushed himself into a seated position as he smirked at his friend. "Jealous?"

"Why would I be jealous of you? You'd lose your head if it wasn't attached." Lucas sat in a nearby chair pulling out his phone mindlessly going through it. "I must say though, Tank, I'm surprised you even know where your phone is."

"I didn't lose my phone, numb-nuts. I couldn't find my keys," Hank corrected as a matter of fact. His shoulders squared, as he stared at his friend, ready for the challenge.

Lucas' eyes lit as a mischievous smile spread across his face. "Rick owes me twenty bucks. Thank you, Hank the Tank."

Hank's eyes hardened. "Fuck you."

"Nah, you ain't my type." Lucas nodded his head toward Hank's device. "What's got you so engrossed there, Tank?"

"Porn," Hank replied without missing a beat.

Lucas laughed before shaking his head. "For looking at porn, you're in a grump ass mood."

He looked back at his phone. Hank couldn't deny it, he was in a mood. Wouldn't anyone be after finding out the woman they've pined over for years fucking writes shit like this?

His eye twitched, and what kind of name was Quinn Sparks?

Sighing he pushed his annoyance down. He still couldn't wrap his head around it. How had he gone so long without knowing? Her first book was published four years ago.

Four. Fucking. Years. Ago.

He had so many questions. Olive Quinn, wallflower, anti-social, curvy as fuck, was a closeted sex goddess extraordinaire.

Closing his eyes, his imagination took on a mind of its own. He pictured himself on the cover of her book. Olive would be on her knees, looking up at him, in his turnout gear. He'd see the lust seeded deeply in her eyes as she begged him to release his *hose*...

"Dude, fuck man, no one wants to see your stiffy." Hank had no time to react before being hit with a magazine. "Put that thing away." Lucas stood cringing.

Hank glanced down his body and sure enough, his pants had a bulge. He wasn't surprised. Olive had always got his body going. However, since finding out about her double life, he clearly was no longer able to control it.

Fuck it, he shrugged.

Lucas walked out of the room, throwing his thumb over his shoulder toward Hank. "Don't go in there unless you want an eyeful of Tank wankin' his little Hank!"

"Fuck you, Luke," Hank hollered after him as he laughed.

Ignoring the commotion coming from the other room, and with a smile on his face, Hank returned to the task at hand.

Hovering his finger over the purchase link, he bought the book. Along with every other book she'd published.

There is so much I don't know about my little Olive Oil, he thought as the books downloaded onto his phone. He clicked on the first one that finished. *But I'm about to find out.*

CHAPTER SEVEN

WELL, this is wonderful...

Olive grumbled as she watched Hank once again come home from his most recent shift with his face buried in his phone and head straight to his bedroom before shutting the door.

Seriously, what the heck?

Her eyes narrowed as she stared at his closed bedroom door. "Well, fuck you too then."

Olive massaged her temples briefly before she grabbed her computer off the coffee table. She didn't know why she bothered. Her concentration on her words had been shot to hell.

She still hadn't figured out what happened between Hank and her. It was like she was non-existent to him now. What happened to all his crap about *I want to have a roommate I actually see, and blah blah blah,* she mocked.

She finally gave in and started venturing out of her room and he up and disappears.

Well, screw you and the horse you rode in on, Hank Parker.

Olive knew she was overreacting, but there was a part of her that was hurt. She had thought things were going better between them. And, truth be told she liked having him around. He gave her an insider scoop on the male personality, and she was eating it up. Who knew having first-hand research would be so beneficial. Too bad that gravy train left and she somehow missed the stop.

Olive huffed before she went back to her computer. There was no sense in getting angry. She'd spent the better part of her life avoiding Hank the stupid Tank, she might as well go back to doing that again.

No matter how scrumptious he looked, or how when he looked at her, his eyes held a heat she wasn't sure existed outside of her books.

Fuck him.

Fuck him in his fuckity face, if he wanted to ignore her effort of being a better roommate then he could go to hell in a handbasket for all she cared.

Going back to her computer she focused on her work. As she read over the last few sentences, her mind started to wander, though. Before she knew it, she was picturing Hank playing out her scenes. His body hard and inviting above her as she pleaded with him to make her his...

Olive closed her eyes when she felt her cheeks heat. Her mind imagined Hank coming out of his bedroom, staring her down as if she were his prey and he was the predator. He'd avidly watch her like she was his only food source.

She shuddered.

He'd already demonstrated his power when he picked her up before throwing her onto the couch on day one.

Her body heated as she bit her bottom lip. *Hank...* Her mind had him stalking toward her.

She felt her nipples tighten as her hand took on a mind of its own and started trailing down her body. She was about to reach her destination when the thump on the couch had her eyes shooting open.

"Ahh!" Her hand went over her chest as she tried focusing on her surroundings.

Dog deliberately sat next to her staring her down as she licked her lips.

Moving a few inches away, Olive's eyes widened. "Good kitty. Nice kitty," Olive tried reassuring the creature.

When Dog opened her mouth to yawn, Olive swore she purposely moved her head from side to side showing off her canines.

Very sharp canines.

Canines Olive never wanted to be acquainted with.

"Dog knock it off."

Olive shot her head toward the voice as she saw Hank come out of his bedroom, shirtless again. His phone still in his hand. Why was he so obsessed with his phone right now? Instantly, her anger rose.

Not only had she let her mind wander to the *danger zone,* but seeing him still glued to his phone sent a wave of hurt through her.

Thankfully, Dog must have taken her owner's warning to heart because she jumped down and strode over to him. As the creature brushed against Hank's legs, he bent petting her between the ears.

I wonder what it would feel like to be pet by him too? She blanched, as her eyebrows shot to the roof. *What the sweet zombie hell did I just say?*

Shaking her head to clear her thoughts she remembered she was mad at him.

Asshole.

Removing her eyes from the cat, she looked at his face. She saw Hank give her the once-over before turning away and heading into the kitchen.

44

He freaking dismissed her *again.*

She looked down at herself. Sure, she was kind of a mess. She'd been on a writing binge. Moving her hand to her hair, she cringed as she remembered she hadn't brushed it in three days. Right now, she was about negative two days on the shower front too. But that didn't give him the right to look down on her. Doing another once-over on herself, she saw her muffin top peeking over her pajama bottoms. She held back her groan.

No fucking wonder.

First, she looked like a complete mess, then she had her excess lumps and bumps on display. Maybe she couldn't blame him for staying clear of her.

Shaking her head, she tried her best to pat down her angry hair. *See this is why I miss Miranda here. I never had to be concerned with my appearance. I wasn't forced to wear a bra, and I could go on three-day writing marathons and not worry about being judged for not taking a shower. But no. Now I've got to look presentable in my own freaking apartment. I have to look prim and proper for Hank the stupid Tank to even acknowledge my presence.*

Screw that. Screw him. And while she was at it, screw his jolly green giant sized cat.

In a quick movement she reached for her drink on the coffee table. That's when she got a good whiff of herself. "Eww." Her nose scrunched in disgust.

Looking around the room she saw Hank still in the kitchen his phone in his face.

As her annoyance started to rise again, she closed her laptop.

Writing was a lost cause. Olive reached for her phone quickly pulling up Miranda's number.

Have I told you lately that I want to murder your brother?

Within seconds she received a reply.

Only about every other day. What did he do now? Or was it Dog? Wait, wait don't tell me. Dog got into your room and stood at the end of your bed sharpening her teeth? What do I win for getting it right?

Olive rolled her eyes.

Let me ship your brother back to you. No returns accepted... No, he's just a pain in my ass. One second, he's all let's be roommates and do things together and the next he's MIA. Which I don't really mind, I'm on a deadline, but whenever I start writing he reappears and screws everything up.

Miranda was quick to reply.

What do you mean he messes with you? Do you want me to give him a stern talking to? What about his hot friends, have they been coming over? Maybe that's your problem.

If she only knew her problem revolved around her wandering mind with Hank and not his friends.

I want it to go back to you being here and not him. I miss the simplicity of it. Come back and save me. I'm needy.

Olive shook her head. Great now Hank had made her needy. She wasn't needy, but now that he was in her life, everything had turned upside down.

Wouldn't it be great if we could go back to when we were younger? Remember all those nights we'd stay up late watching horror movies and place bets on who was gonna die first?

A smile appeared on Olive's face.

Those were the good old days. The days before Hank the Tank and his monster cat showed up.

When Olive received the eye roll emoji, she quickly replied.

What? It's the truth and you know it.

Olive pushed herself back into the couch.

It's not that bad, you and I both know it. I've got to head back into work but call me tonight. And, remember, you've got a plethora of hot men to stare at from the station. Make this momma proud and go bring them some cookies and be sure to report back every detail to me.

Olive shook her head with a laugh, before she typed out her reply.

You are unbelievable.

She got a reply within seconds.

But you love me.

Olive couldn't deny it.

I do.

Putting her phone on the coffee table, Olive stood. She stretched her arms to the ceiling, as she tried to work out her stiff muscles.

Glancing at Hank with the corner of her eye, she sighed.

She couldn't fix whatever was going on between her and Hank, and she couldn't fix how forced her words seemed in her latest project, but she could fix one thing.

One last glance toward Hank had her shaking her head in anger.

Whatever. A shower would do me good.

———

Hank's jaw clenched as he watched Olive walk from the living room to the bathroom. The sway in her hips had his mouth watering.

Closing his eyes, he recalled the little stretch she did after getting up from the couch. Her shirt had risen a few inches giving him the smallest tease of her skin.

Sweat started to form on his brow as he held back his groan. He'd give anything to walk over to her, fall to his knees and finally get his first taste of her skin.

He was hanging on by a thread. A fragile thread. A thread that if she looked his way one more time was liable to snap.

Taking a deep breath to control his body he looked down at his phone.

For the last four days every spare moment he had was consumed with reading Olive's books. Every. Single. One. Of. Them.

After starting the first one at the station, he couldn't put it down. Not only did it possess a plot line that made him want to know what happened next, but they were hot. Really hot. Actually, hot wasn't the right word. They were downright sexy as fuck.

He'd taken more cold showers in the last four days than he had in his entire life.

Not to mention the amount of times he had to relieve

himself throughout the day, he was completely raw. At this point, he was worried his dick would start to chafe.

When he came in from work and saw her on the couch, he had to bite back the urge to run to her. He was in the middle of reading a scene in her, "I'm Yours to Command," series that had the hero standing over his heroine. Her arms and legs were tied giving the hero an open invitation to her body. His mind couldn't help but replace the characters with him and Olive.

The way Olive wrote the scene had his dick threatening to break free once again. He had to hightail it into his room or risk her seeing his hard on.

It took him a few minutes, but once he got his wayward cock under control, he ventured out of the bedroom to finally say hello to her.

That's when he saw Dog once again showing her dominance over Olive.

Fuck. He'd like to show his dominance over Olive too.

After Dog reluctantly came to him he looked up to see Olive staring right at him. Her hair was a little messy, and her clothes were wrinkled. He examined her body further noticing her cheeks held a hint of red, as her breasts rose and fell with her breathing.

Without pause, his lower half had tightened. Olive Quinn looked like she'd been well and utterly fucked, and fucked hard.

It took everything in him to turn away from her and head to the kitchen.

As he busied himself looking for food, his mind wouldn't shut off. He one hundred and fucking ten percent wouldn't mind a little role play if that was her kink. And who wouldn't want to see her tied to his bed at his mercy?

This time he didn't hold back his groan.

Tossing his phone onto the counter he did his best to

tamper down his lust. This needed to stop. This was Olive Quinn, his little sister's best friend.

But, Olive Quinn was also his fantasy come to life, her curves beckoned him, and her smart mouth had him coming alive.

Fuck he needed to figure out his game plan and fast. He was done with waiting.

Taking a deep breath, he stretched out his body.

Looking at his phone he felt his body tighten. Scenes from her books played in his mind. Sweet, innocent Olive Quinn had a dirty as fuck mind.

A grin ran across his face.

Dog purred at his feet, pulling him from his thoughts. "I don't know if I should," he said, reaching down to pluck the cat into his arms. "Didn't we talk about intimidating Olive?"

The cat blinked at him before purring again. "None of this sweet talk, missy."

He put Dog back on the floor before retrieving her food. "No more, you hear me?"

The moment he placed the cat food on the floor he heard an earth-shattering scream. His natural instincts went into full force as he took off toward the bathroom.

CHAPTER EIGHT

As THE WATER ran down Olive's body, she couldn't help but let her annoyance and hurt of the situation overtake her. She knew Hank living with her was going to be a problem, she just didn't fully comprehend the extent of it.

Living with him was like permanently living on a roller coaster. And that was a life she didn't want to live.

Plus, it hurt.

Ultimately, that annoyed her more than anything. She shouldn't hurt because Hank finally realized he had better things to do than spend time with her. And it sure as hell shouldn't hurt when he looked at her body and then blatantly dismissed her.

No.

She'd long since realized other people's opinions of her should not matter.

When Josh... she shuddered at the name. When he humiliated her by telling everyone they knew how lousy she was in bed, or how he'd have to take a deep breath in fear of being suffocated when he was with her, she promised herself she'd never feel that kind of worthlessness again.

She was perfect goddamn it, and if anyone had a problem with that it was on them, not her.

But here she was again.

Olive just didn't know why this time it hurt worse.

Pushing away her betrayal and hurt, she took a calming breath. Olive prided herself on being a strong person. Just like the women she wrote about. That's why as soon as she got wind of what Josh was saying and doing, she hightailed it over to him and slapped him in the face. No one was going to publicly humiliate her and walk away unscathed.

Nonetheless, that was one of the last times she ever went to a party. Parties weren't safe. Hell, people weren't safe. Humans were assholes, and human interaction was the absolute worst thing possible.

You can't trust humans, time and time again that was proven to her. In order to shield their own insecurities, they'd find someone else to sling their hate at. Somehow, she was always that person. From her parents always telling their friends she was a disappointment, to Josh preaching how he threw himself on the sword to even sleep with her.

See people were assholes.

After Josh, she promised herself she'd never let another person shame her.

She groaned as the water ran over her skin. She placed her head on the shower wall before she lightly smacked it. *You're doing so well on your promise to yourself, Olive. Oh, so freaking well. Idiot.*

She didn't know how or why it happened, but Hank somehow got under her skin.

And not the under your skin that would go away eventually. No, this was the under your skin that felt like poisonous caterpillars had decided on making you their host, and you can't do anything but let them have their way with you as they eat you alive from the inside out.

"Stupid Hank," she mumbled as she reached for the body wash. "Stupid cat." Her anger started to rise even higher. "Stupid everything." After putting some of the body wash in her hands, she slammed the container back onto the side of the tub. "And stupid freaking body for constantly responding to Hank the stupidest of stupid Tank!"

Olive started angrily washing her skin as she looked at the ceiling. "I swear to all things, Universe, if you have any ounce of mercy in you, please send down your alien minions to take Hank back to their leader." Narrowing her eyes at the ceiling she continued, "Or hell, take me for all I care."

Her lips thinned while she continued her task. "And why the hell doesn't he ever wear a shirt? Seriously, a shirt is a barrier against the elements. A shirt should *always* be worn. It's science. Duh."

As she grumbled in her angry fantasy, her mind took a turn. *Out of nowhere, she pictured Hank in all his glory coming out of his bedroom, shirtless no doubt. And he was headed right toward her. "What are you doing, Olive?" he asked, before looking her up and down. When she looked into his eyes, she saw pure heat. Her breath hitched at the intensity she saw there. "Nothing, Hank. Just getting something to drink and making a snack."*

Hank licked his lips before pushing himself off the wall and purposely walking toward her. "What a coincidence. I came out here to get a snack too." Olive turned to face him. "Oh, really?" He stopped a few inches from her. "Yes, really. Only difference is you're *my snack."*

The shower water felt heated against her skin. She couldn't stop her body's reaction to her fantasy even if she tried. Instead, Olive let her hand glide down her curves as she sought out her core.

This is Hank, your best friend's brother and the guy that's turned your world upside down. Stop! Her mind tried to protest, but quickly lost the battle when her fantasy moved to Hank falling to his knees in front of her.

Olive was so caught up in her fantasy, she didn't realize her body had started leaning. Right as she was about to hit her peak, her shoulder hit the wall causing a jolt of surprise to shoot through her. She flailed around hitting all of the bottles off the ledge causing her to scream in shock as she toppled over.

Hank burst through the bathroom door, his adrenaline working overtime. Dread washed through him as he scanned the room, looking for anything that could confirm Olive was not in danger.

Blame his firefighter instincts. He didn't care. He couldn't count the number of times he'd gone into a situation thinking everything would be fine, for all hell to break loose.

Taking a few steps toward the shower he threw open the curtain and jumped in. "Olive, are you okay? What happened, are you hurt?" He fell to his knees as he saw Olive in a pile on the shower floor, with miscellaneous bottles flung all over the place.

Within seconds he was moving her around examining her body for any sign of injury.

"Get out!"

Olive slammed her arms over her chest. "Hank, get out now!" she repeated.

Hank blinked a few times trying to register Olive's movements with hiding her body. Why in the hell was she so stubborn? Didn't she understand he was checking her over to make sure she wasn't hurt? Shaking his head, he started to examine her again. "Not until you tell me you're okay," he growled with annoyance. *Stupid fickle woman.*

"I'm fine, now get out!" Her hand went to the back of her head causing Hank's focus on where she could be injured. He threw his left leg over her hips, straddling her to get a better angle. He then pulled her head closer to his face.

"I said get out, not dry hump me."

"I'd be wet humping seeing as the shower is still on," he ground out before examining her head. "It doesn't look like it's bleeding. Where did you hit it?"

"Hank Parker, I swear to all things, get out of this shower right now. I'm freakin' naked!"

If her being naked was her biggest concern then he was going to fix that. "Oh, for fuck's sake." He grabbed the waistband of his basketball shorts he'd thrown on after work and pushed them off his body. "See, I'm naked too. Now, tell me what the hell happened?" His eyes narrowed at her. If she wanted to be a pain in his ass, then he was going to be a pain in hers.

He moved his examination down her body, making sure she was in fact okay. After doing a preliminary scan he looked back at her eyes. That's when he noticed they were wide, frightful, and also zoned in on one thing.

If this were another time he would have laughed. He'd dreamed about Olive witnessing his dick for the first time for years. Her being sprawled out on the shower floor, clinging to her head was not how he imagined it happening. Leave it to Olive to always keep him on his toes.

Ignoring the lust building in her eyes as she took in his dick, he moved his attention back to the situation. "Olive," he spoke a little softer. "Tell me you're not hurt. Or if so, where?"

Hank watched as she forcefully removed her eyes from in between his legs and looked at him. "I'm... no... I'm not hurt." She swallowed.

Knowing she was out of danger he let out a breath he didn't realize he was holding.

The reality of the situation started to sink in.

Right now, he was in the shower with a naked Olive Quinn. He was just as naked, sans the shorts around his knees. His eyes slowly scanned her body more appreciatively. He didn't even try to hide his body's reaction.

Olive's breasts were full, just the way he liked them, far more than a handful. Her nipples were a dusty pink, that called to him. It took everything inside of him not to bend down and finally get a taste of her. Unfortunately, her lower half was covered with his own body, so he moved his gaze back to her face.

What he saw almost knocked the breath out of him.

Lust stared back at him.

Lust for *him*.

Finally!

In one movement, he had his hands on her waist lifting her in the shower. He placed her on her feet, turning her away from him.

"What, what are you doing?" she breathlessly asked as he started moving his hands all over her body exploring every inch of her.

"I'm making sure you don't have any cuts on your back." This was the moment he'd been waiting for all his life. He wasn't about to miss this opportunity.

Moving all of Olive's hair to her shoulder he started at her neck. Using his fingertips, he gently traced down the curve.

He placed his other hand on her hip and squeezed causing her to hitch her breath. He squeezed again causing her body to grind into his. Bringing his lips to her ear, he whispered, "Now, that I know you're not hurt, Olive. It's time to clean you up." He reached around her grabbing the body wash that had somehow escaped catastrophe. He brought his other arm around her, plastering his front to her back. Squeezing some soap into his palm, he threw the bottle down, before he brought his hands together.

Feeling her body pressed against his, had every last one of his nerve endings on fire. He'd never been harder than he was right now in his life, and he knew Olive could feel every inch of him. There was no hiding it, and frankly he didn't want to. Not when his fantasy girl was standing in front of him. Her lush curves, pressed against his body, enticing him.

"Okay," she moaned.

Hearing her voice sent a new shockwave through his body. He couldn't wait a second longer. He brought his hands to her breasts cupping them before he slowly started to lather them. Using one of his hands, he found her nipple and began to tweak it, while his left hand started trailing down her stomach.

"Yes," she whispered as she pushed her ass against his groin, signaling for him to continue.

That was all he needed.

His predatory instincts took over.

Turning her around to face him, he pushed her against the tile wall before sealing his lips to hers. Her hands frantically roamed his body as he explored her mouth with his.

Their kiss ignited him. It was unlike any other kiss he'd ever had. "Touch me," he growled into her mouth.

His own hands started exploring her, as he did his best to memorize every inch. He lost count of the time's he'd imagined her body, and there was no way in hell he was missing the chance to not commit her lush curves to memory.

Breaking away from her mouth he turned her once again, before pushing on her back, forcing her to bend at the waist.

"I'm clean." He gritted his teeth, as he traced her skin with his fingertips. "We have to be checked every three months at the station."

"Me too," she said, looking over her shoulder at him. The urgency in her eyes almost unmanned him. "I mean, I don't have to get checked at the station, but I'm clean. I haven't been with anyone since—"

"Don't say his name," Hank swore. *Fuck that asshole.* He was about to make sure she forgot his name. Grabbing the base of his dick he lined it up with her pussy.

Fuck, she had the most perfect pussy he'd ever seen. It was full, just like the rest of her and lightly trimmed. He wanted to sink to his knees and bury his face there, but that was going to have to wait for another time.

Even through the water of the shower he could see her glistening with need for him.

Dragging his cock against her slit again he enticed a moan from her. *That's right baby, moan for me. Only me.*

Olive pushed back against him, trying to force his hand and enter her. "Not yet, Olive. You need to learn who's in charge here."

"Hank, please," she begged, before slamming her ass against him.

He liked the sound of that. Her begging for him. He was damn sure going to make it his mission for Olive to always beg for him. Squeezing her ass with his free hand, he moved his dick so the tip was inside of her. Her tight walls clamped around the head causing him to throw back his head and groan. "Olive, my sweet Olive, please tell me you are on the pill?" He felt like he was seconds from snapping.

"Yes!" she screamed.

"Thank fuck." He never wanted to be inside of Olive with a barrier.

Never.

Picking her left knee up, he placed it in the crevice of his arm giving him the perfect angle to enter her.

"Jesus Hank, I thought they called you Tank for a reason?

Stop messing around and fuck me!" she growled, before she pushed her ass all the way back causing him to enter her fully.

The sensation of her tight walls clamping around him shot his every nerve ending on fire. He spanked her. "You're a naughty girl. I will punish you for that." He spanked her again, loving the way her ass jiggled around him.

She pushed back once again causing him to enter even farther into her. "You're already punishing me by not fucking me. Come on, Hank. Fuck me."

"Oh, you're asking for it," he said, moving inside of her painfully slow. He was in charge, not her.

"No, I'm begging for it."

Her words sent a new wave of possessiveness over him. He pushed onto her back making her bend at the waist even more before thrusting inside of her with a rapid force.

If she wanted to be fucked, he was damn sure going to give it to her. Every last fucking inch.

"Yes!" she screamed as he moved inside of her with more force. "Harder! Hank, now!"

Who was he to deny her? He increased his movements, as her walls clamped down on him. Her wet heat almost burned him as pleasure surged throughout his body.

Dropping her leg, he straightened her, before moving one of his hands to her core, the other wrapped around her chest keeping her in place as he pounded into her.

The second he found her clit, he pinched it causing her to scream in pleasure.

"That's right come for me, Olive. Come now."

As her body convulsed around him, he felt his orgasm take hold. He thrust one more time before emptying himself deep inside of her.

CHAPTER NINE

As Olive finally started to get her breathing under control the reality of the situation sunk in.

Holy crapolie! Olive's eyes widened when she realized Hank was still inside of her. *Oh my God. Oh my God. What do I do?*

Hank freakin' Parker.

Hank of all people had his manwhore dick buried inside. Of. Her. *Oh shit!*

What the hell had she just done?

One step at a time, Olive. Taking a deep breath, she pushed her hips forward. It took everything in her not to moan when she felt Hank slip out of her. Seriously, what in the hell was wrong with her? *Good going, Olive. Please add this to your list of mess-ups.*

Her heart started to race as her chest tightened. Refusing to look behind her, because lord knows, *nothing* good would come out of seeing Hank's face, she tried to figure out her next move.

Get to bedroom.

Lock bedroom door.

Die.

Sounds reasonable enough.

Now to figure out a way to get past Hank and put her plan into action.

However, it seemed as though Hank had other plans. The moment she lifted her hand to push the shower curtain back she felt his arm wrap around her midsection pulling her close to his body.

Well, okay then.

Feeling Hank move behind her, sent a new wave of desire through her. Too bad it was accompanied by a new wave of panic. *Oh, come the freak on, body. Get a hold of yourself.*

As she tried calculating her next move she felt him lean into her before brushing his lips against her neck.

Then he was gone.

Olive stood there in the shower in utter and complete shock.

Finally taking the chance she looked behind her, and sure enough, Hank was nowhere to be found.

Did he really think he could stick it in me then leave without even a word? She didn't know why, but that pissed her off. *That was my plan, not his! If anyone was doin' the bang and bounce it was me. I called it.* Hank didn't get to play out *her* plan. Even if that meant marching straight into his bedroom and dragging his ass back into the shower so she could be the one to leave *him.* Well, then so be it.

Stupid Hank.

She turned off the water, as her mind raced with what had just transpired. *This is what you wanted, Olive. Stop being angry. You can go back to living in your room and in your fantasy world.* She could buy one of those small fridges, and live out of her room. Only coming out when she knew Hank was at the station.

This could work. *See, plans are easy.* She mentally pat herself on the back. *Crisis averted.*

Olive pulled back the curtain with a smile on her face and a bounce in her step. Too bad it was short-lived. Her mouth fell open in shock when she saw Hank waiting for her. Her favorite fluffy towel wrapped around his waist.

Her eyes narrowed. *Stupid. Freaking. Hank.* And, how dare he use her towel. Just because he was inside of her, does not give him the right. Oh God, Hank Parker had been inside of her... Olive's eyes widened.

"I was wondering what was taking you so long," he said, grabbing another towel from the rack. Before she could say anything, he wrapped her in it.

Within seconds she was out of the tub standing in front of him as he started to dry her off. As her mind tried to register the fact Hank had once again picked her up so effortlessly, she stood there dumbly letting him do whatever he wanted.

He was ruthless. Hank dried every inch of her body. The towel skimmed lightly across her arms, legs, breasts, all with ease as he made sure to reach every crevice of her body.

Her very naked body.

She snatched the towel from him, as she covered herself. "What the hell do you think you're doing?"

He quirked his left brow. "Drying you. What does it look like I'm doing?" Reaching for the towel he easily pulled it from her grip and continued his task. "Spread your legs."

Her whole body crimsoned. "You are not drying my who-ha."

Hank quirked his eyebrow. "Don't be so stubborn."

Olive's body being exposed was instantly forgotten. She placed her hands on her hips and looked him square in the eye. "*I'm* the one that's stubborn? Have you met yourself?"

Hank barked out a laugh "You're cute when you try and act tough. Now, let me dry you."

Did he have a death wish?

She stared at him wide-eyed. There was no way in hell someone could convince her this was *not* some sort of alternate universe. Looking around the tiny bathroom once again, she felt Hank move the towel between her legs.

"That's enough of that." She stepped away from him.

Hank shifted back before he burst out laughing. "Olive Oil, what am I gonna do with you?"

"Absolutely nothing." Grabbing the towel, she wrapped it around her body before dashing off to her room. She'd make sense of what corner of hell she'd just come from later.

She only made it as far as the door before she found herself in the air flung over Hank's shoulder. "Let me go you big oaf."

"Not on your life."

———

The moment Hank saw Olive make a run for it, he let his instincts take over. There was no way in hell he would let her retreat to her room.

Especially, not after he finally got a taste of her.

It'd be a cold day in hell before he let her slip past him.

Bouncing her on his shoulder making her sturdier, he smirked. He did his best to hold in his laughter as he felt her flailing around. Without even a second thought he smacked her ass, causing her to still instantly.

"Did you just smack my butt?" she growled.

"Yup." He did it again for good measure.

Olive started pounding on his back. "I will kill you. Mark my words, Hank Parker, the second you let me down prepare for my fury."

This time he did laugh not caring anymore. "I'm looking forward to it." And boy was he ever. An angry Olive was a fun Olive in his eyes.

Keeping his hand on her ass, he took a step into the bedroom, his eyes spotting Dog on the foot of his bed instantly. The cat looked at him, then Olive, before yawning. "Move it, young lady," he remarked.

I don't need your innocent eyes seeing what I'm about to do to your soon to be mommy.

"I can't move anything you Neanderthal until you put me down."

Hank smacked her ass again, before smirking. "I wasn't talking to you. I was talking to Dog."

Her whole body stiffened as he felt Olive actually try to climb up his body searching for the high ground. "Where is it? Is it going to attack? Oh God, my ass is in the air. It's like the perfect target for the she-devil."

Hank smacked her ass again, causing Olive to jump. "Stop calling Dog names."

"Tell her to stop trying to eat me!"

"Only one pussy is getting eaten tonight and it has nothing to do with Dog." Hank tossed Olive onto the bed and watched her bounce a few inches, causing her towel to fall open.

She'd never looked more beautiful than she had at this exact moment. With all of her curves entirely on display it made his mouth water.

Her face was flushed, and her breathing was ragged, causing her breasts to rise and fall.

He needed her.

At this point he didn't think he could survive without her.

Hank threw the towel from around his waist onto the floor before he slowly crawled up the bed toward Olive.

Her eyes widened, as her cheeks heated.

That's right, baby.

He loved seeing the desire in her eyes. It egged him on like nothing else. Her whole face filled with a lust he craved.

When he was halfway up the bed, Olive's legs fell to their sides, giving him the access, he sought.

Looking between her legs, he was greeted with the most perfect view of her core. A core, he was about to get well acquainted with.

Instinctively, he wiped his chin. *Wait, am I drooling?* He looked back at her plump pussy.

Yeah, he was probably drooling.

As he lowered himself between her legs, his face only inches from her center, he looked into her eyes that were filled with need which he was sure matched his own. "Silly Olive, did you really think I was done with you?"

CHAPTER TEN

HANK FELL to the bed after emptying himself inside of Olive once again. *Fuck, I could get used to this,* he thought as he worked to get his breathing under control.

Once Olive let go, she fucking came alive. She gave as good as she got. Hell, this could be his new workout.

Hank licked his lips.

The taste of her pussy was something he wanted to feast on for the rest of his goddamn life. She was the perfect combination of salty and sweet. And when he sunk into her, it was like nothing he'd ever felt before.

Olive Quinn. Sex goddess.

He smiled at the memory of him behind her. He didn't think he'd ever rode someone as hard as he did her.

She's made for me.

Closing his eyes, he let his body relax in the moment. That was until he felt the stubborn woman move out of his grasp.

Opening his left eye, he saw Olive bend and pick up her towel before placing it securely around herself.

"Where do you think you're going?" he asked, pushing

himself onto his elbows. He cocked his brow at her when he saw her shy away from him.

"My room."

Pushing himself fully upright, he stared at her retreating form. There was no way in hell he could let her leave this room. He knew the second she did, he'd lose her. "Why?"

She turned and faced him. Her mouth was slightly open, and her eyes wide. "Did you really just ask why?"

"I didn't stutter."

"No," she agreed with annoyance. "You didn't."

Hank crossed his arms over his chest. If she wanted to play this game he would be more than willing to participate. "Then answer me. Why are you trying to sneak out?"

She rolled her eyes while she placed one of her hands on her hip. "I'm not sneaking out. If I were sneaking out I would have tiptoed out of here. Instead, I rolled over, grabbed my towel and *walked*. No sneaking involved."

Oh, he was going to like this. He gave her a half smile. "If you weren't trying to sneak out, why won't you look me in the eyes?"

"I am looking you in the eyes."

"No," he stated. "You're looking at my chin."

The spark of annoyance that ran over her features had him holding back his laugh. He loved being able to rile her so easy.

"I'm going back to my room."

One thing he knew for certain about Olive Quinn was that she never backed down from a challenge. "Olive, look at me," he said sternly, putting the challenge in his voice.

"Fine," she huffed. Her eyes reluctantly moved to his. "What do you want?"

The fire he saw in her made his mouth curve into a smile. This was the feisty Olive he loved. The Olive that would tell you how you were an idiot without even batting an eye. "Drop your towel," he demanded.

"No."

"Yes."

Throwing her hands in the air, Olive spun on her heel ready to storm off to her room. "That's it, I'm out of here."

His excitement of the situation grew. He knew exactly what he needed to do.

"Quinn Sparks wouldn't leave."

Olive froze.

What did he just say? She turned slowly. That's when she saw his face in a wide grin.

"Excuse me." She paused. "What did you say?" she asked calmly praying she'd heard him wrong.

She knew she hadn't with his whole face lit in mischief.

Oh, crap on a stick! Taking a deep breath, she took a step closer to him.

"You heard me, Olive Oil, or should I say Quinn Sparks." He winked at her. The fucker actually winked at her. She didn't know whether to cry or run. She knew what was coming next. It was always the same when someone found out what she did. They'd laugh in her face, go out of their way to make jabs about her, then they'd assume she was some weird sex freak and that she was easy-

Wait a minute.

Olive's mouth fell open. "You fucking asshole!" She leaped into the air, her target acquired.

"Whoa, Olive." Hank caught her in mid-flight. "What the hell has gotten into you?"

She ignored him as she tried her best to pull out of his grasp, so she could turn around and beat the crap out of him.

How dare he use her. Just because she wrote sexy books did not mean her body was an open invitation.

Screw him.

The second she got back to her room she was calling Miranda and letting her have it. Her stupid brother had ruined her life.

Hank squeezed her tighter, which only pissed Olive off more. Looking around she saw her knee was right next to his man junk.

Seeing her opportunity, she pulled her knee back.

"No, you don't." Hank's hand stopped her knee from hitting her target only frustrating her more. In fear for his junk, he let go of her to cover his man meat... Albeit, man meat she would need to store into her memory to use for one of her characters later.... *Seriously, how in the hell did that thing even fit inside of me?* Ignoring her wayward thoughts, she took her chance and punched Hank right in the jaw.

That'll teach the jerk.

"What the fuck?" he hollered, letting go of his dick to cup where she'd hit him.

Seeing her chance for escape, Olive jumped back grabbing her towel that had flown off in her attempt to dive bomb him and flung it around her tightly. "If you thought for one second I'd be easy 'cause you found out what I do for a living, you are sorely mistaken, Hank Parker. That was a dirty thing for you to do. I know you've never really liked me, but that was beyond wrong." Anger coursed through her body. If she thought what Josh had done was bad, this was ten times worse.

This was unforgivable.

"What the fuck are you blabbering about?" Hank asked, still rubbing his jaw.

"You know exactly what I'm talking about. You somehow found out what I write and wanted to see if I was a sex-crazed freak." She jabbed her finger in his direction. "Let me tell you something, Hank. I write love stories. Stories that pull emotions out of people and their lives. Sex is a part of life. Therefore, it goes into my books!" she yelled.

Screw this and screw him.

Olive turned ready to leave. She'd deal with what to do later, but right now she needed to get the hell away from *him*.

How in the heck could she have been so stupid?

This was all his fault. His shirtlessness made my brain dumb. Shirtless sexy men, make otherwise sensible women's minds go to mush.

"I know. I read them," Hank announced.

She froze.

Hank really read her books?

Slowly, she turned to face him, her gut clenched. The second she saw the humor in his eyes, she'd lose it.

She was wrong.

No humor stared back at her. Her heart slammed against her chest. Instead of humor, she saw something completely different...

Olive watched in awe, as Hank jumped off the bed and moved toward her, a predatory gleam in his eyes. "I've spent the last few days reading every single one of your books, Olive."

His eyes drilled into her. "I've always thought you were sexy. Those curves you keep hidden away could make a grown man fall to his knees." His eyes scanned her body. "I've wanted to sink into you for as long as I can remember." He licked his lips before he continued, "When I found out you had this secret side of you, it only made me want you more. My sweet little Olive Oil has a side of her that's begging to be explored." He stood directly in front of her causing her to back up to the wall. "But mark my words, Olive Quinn. Even if you only edited textbooks, I'd still want to bend you over right now and fuck you until you scream my name. Your writing doesn't change how bad I've wanted you. It's only icing on the cake." He placed his hands on either side of her head, boxing her in.

Hank's presence was more than she could handle. Situations like this only happened in the stories she wrote about.

Never in real life.

Closing her eyes, she did what she always did best. She started compartmentalizing his words. This was nothing more than a dream or nightmare, whichever way you wanted to look at it.

Maybe, just maybe, I really have been transported to an alien planet.

"No, you're right here with *me,* Olive. I'm not some alien creature your twisted, but sexy as fuck mind came up with."

Olive rapidly blinked at him a few times. Had she said those words out loud? *Crap on a stick.*

Hank laughed before she watched his features soften. He gently placed his forehead on hers. "How's your head, Olive? Are you sore anywhere?"

Her face scrunched. Did he want to know if her who-ha was sore? Who asks that? *See this is why I avoid human interaction. Shit gets weird.*

"That crash sounded loud when you fell earlier. You don't have any pain, right?"

Oh. She mentally hit her forehead. He was talking about the wayward fantasy involving the bane of her existence that lead to all of this mess. A mess that included getting boinked by the person causing her frustrations.

Taking a calming breath, she did her best to ignore his close proximity. "I'm fine."

Was she really fine, though?

Hell freaking no.

She desperately needed to retreat back to her room to try

71

and make sense of all of this. Maybe she could make a rope out of her sheets like she'd seen in prison escapes and make a run for it from her window.

It could work.

Who was she kidding? It wouldn't work. With her luck, the sheet would come undone the moment she put her weight on it.

As she tried to come up with a plan that didn't involve her falling to her death, Hank's voice broke through her thoughts.

"When did you start writing?" he asked, moving away from her before he sat at the end of the bed, giving her some space.

Her brows pulled together. "Oh no, how about you tell me when and how you found out?" she countered.

"The other day, I was looking for my keys and you had your computer on the coffee table. I read a few paragraphs and then everything clicked. Then, I looked you up." His whole face lit. "I must say, I'm pretty impressed. I've been reading your books ever since." When he winked at her, her idiot knees wobbled. "I especially liked your firefighter story. I pictured you were writing about me." The smug look he gave her made her lips thin. "Although, no sane person would put on their bunker pants and suspenders without a shirt on. That's asking for chaffed nipples. Not to mention how unprofessional it would be."

Ground open up and swallow me whole. I'm begging you. Or better yet, send in the zombies. I'm waiting. How dim-witted had she been to leave her laptop in plain sight? She knew better.

Cursing herself, she started to pace the room. "Now you know my secret. Wonderful. Abso-fucking-lutely wonderful. I've spent the better part of my adult life hiding what I do. I cover all my tracks, I keep to myself and then I somehow get complacent with you here and my careless self leaves my laptop out and bam you find out."

She continued to pace through the room, thinking about how she can reverse any damage she was sure Hank would cause her.

"Why do you need to hide it?" he asked. She was taken aback by the sincerity in his voice.

Ignoring it, she snapped her head in his direction. "You've met my parents. Do you honestly think they'd do okay with this? Hell Hank, they threw a "sorry our daughter is a disappointment" party after I declared a degree in English Literature."

Hank's face hardened. "That was a dick move. I never liked how they berated you in front of people."

"You're preaching to the choir there, Bub."

The way her parents acted wasn't new to her. From when she was a child to now, it never changed. When she was younger any free time she got, she spent it at the Parker household. It was safer there. Even with Hank continually making her the butt of his jokes, it was better than being with her parents. They'd either ignore her or if they weren't ignoring her, they were constantly telling her how she was worthless. If she wasn't going to be a lawyer or a doctor to carry on the Quinn name in an honorable way she wasn't good enough for them. End of story.

Olive blanched.

No. She was not going to go back down that path again. She long since accepted her fate when it came to her parents. And right now, she had bigger fish to fry.

Like the fact that she slept with her best friend's brother.

Twice.

And the worst part was... she liked it.

She liked it a hell of a lot.

That was another can of worms she was going to have to deal with once she escaped from her room and boarded a plane to Mexico, never to be seen again. She'll deal with those feelings there.

Olive shook her head before she looked down at her body. *Oh, shit crackers.* Why the hell was she still naked?

Her lumps and bumps were just hanging out in the open for all of the world to see. *Oh God,* she was in the middle of having a naked fight with her best friend's brother who was just as naked as she was.

A naked fight. Who the hell has naked fights?

Her nakedness thoughts were interrupted when Hank spoke. "Don't worry about what your parents think, Olive. They're uptight assholes. I've read your books. You're good."

Not sure what to say, and feeling uncomfortable, Olive crossed her arms over her chest, shielding at least some of her dignity. She nodded. "Thanks, I think."

"Does Miranda know what you do?"

Olive bent down and picked up her favorite towel before placing it around her body. "Yeah, she's the one that encouraged me to write in the first place. She also helps me when I have plot holes or if I'm having a hard time working through a scene."

Hank observed her, his head slightly cocked. "You spend most of your time writing, don't you?"

"For the most part. Although the past couple of weeks I've been in this weird funk. None of my words are coming out right. I can't seem to get any of the characters to speak to me." She'd never felt more vulnerable in her life. Miranda was the only person she talked about her writing with. Right now, she felt like Hank had opened her up and was examining all her insides.

"What's been distracting you from your writing?" he asked softly.

Why is he talking to me like this with his twig and berries just hanging out in the open?

She felt her face heat. *Jesus, Olive, how in the hell did you get yourself into his mess?*

Her eyes scanned his body again. *Oh, for Pete's sake, stop looking at it!*

See Hank had been a distraction since he moved in. It was his fault her words stopped flowing. And now that they've bumped uglies she doubted she'd ever get herself back on track.

The corners of Hank's mouth lifted. "I don't know what the blush means, but I like it. I also like knowing you blush from head to toe."

His words caused her face to heat more. *Anytime now universe. I'm waiting.*

"What do you normally do when you are stuck?"

Olive shrugged. "It depends where I am stuck at. If it's character development, I make charts, if it's a plot twist that has been upside down, I call Miranda. If it's the sex, I watch porn." The moment the words were out of her mouth she groaned. *For fuck's sake, Olive. Did I really just say that?*

Hank cleared his throat. "Porn, huh? I can dig it."

"I'm glad you approve." She rolled her eyes.

"Where are you right now? What are you stuck on?"

Swallowing she looked down at her feet. "You know, I think I've decided I'm done with this conversation."

As she turned away Hank called out. "Olive wait, hear me out. Maybe I can help."

Her brows shot to the ceiling. "How?"

"You already know I want you. I've told you that, you've also just told me when you're stuck you do research." He leaned back on the bed, giving her the perfect view of his body. She'd be foolish not to do a quick lookie loo, so she did.

"I've been pretty busy working doubles at the station," Hank continued, ignoring her perusal of his body. "I haven't had any *me* time. Maybe we can both help each other out?"

"Again, how?"

A smug look ran across Hank's face. "I let you have complete access to my body for your research, and in turn I get sex."

Olive rolled her eyes. "You've got to be kidding me?"

"I'm not. We already know we're good together. Let's see where this goes."

She looked at him dumbfounded. "That is a horrible idea."

Pushing himself upright, he looked her in the eyes. "Do you like when my dick is inside of you? How about my tongue?"

She couldn't answer him.

"Use me for your research, Olive." Hank had a smug look on his face.

Why am I even considering this? she asked herself. Her eyes moved to his dick. *That's why.*

She placed her finger on her chin. Could she use him? This was Hank after all. It wasn't like they hadn't already done it. And until now, she forgot how much she missed sex.

Plus, sex with Hank was fun.

Her mind started racing, Miranda did say Hank would be perfect research material. On the upside, this would save her computer from getting any more viruses.

"If we do this, we do it on my terms," she announced.

"Your terms," he agreed. "But, I have some terms too."

She crossed her arm over her chest. "And what might that be?"

"We do this with each other only. You don't sleep with anyone else and I won't sleep with anyone else."

She stared at him. That wasn't going to be a problem for her, it was more likely to be a problem for him. She took a deep breath while her mind replayed the heroines in her stories. They were always so sure of themselves, and they never turned down an opportunity in fear of the reper-cussions.

They were strong.

They were determined, and she wanted to be like them.

"Fine," she huffed, before taking a step closer to him. "But, we are keeping this a secret. No one finds out. Not even Miranda."

Hank grinned as he leaned back on the bed. He crossed his hands behind his head before crossing his ankles. "Deal. Now drop your towel."

CHAPTER ELEVEN

IT HAD BEEN five days since Hank and Olive agreed on their arrangement. And, it had been a whirlwind for her ever since.

Like right now. Olive had no idea how she ended up agreeing to go to a cookout the fire station was hosting at a nearby park. Yet here she was, in the car, sitting next to an extremely smug Hank.

The jerk.

Albeit, a sexy jerk, but still a jerk.

One moment she was in the living room writing, and the next Hank was between her legs asking her to accompany him. What was she supposed to say? He could have asked her to shave Dog and in that moment she would have agreed.

He played dirty and they both knew it.

So, now here she was in the car being forced to participate in human interaction. *Gahh,* she shuddered at the thought. She needed someone to explain to her how her life had literally been turned upside down and so fast.

Thank God she was getting sex out of the deal now.

Sex that was used against her to agree to go to this cookout.

Olive huffed before crossing her arms over her chest as she sunk further into her seat.

"It's not going to be that bad," Hank said, drawing her from her thoughts.

She snapped her head toward him. "Says you. You know all these people. I'm going to stick out like a sore thumb." Olive fell further into the seat.

"You know some of the guys, Olive. They helped me move in."

Yes, how could Olive forget the shirtless firemen that moved him and *the creature* in? She narrowed her eyes at him. "I don't know them, know them," she grumbled.

Rolling his eyes, Hank turned back to the road. "I'd say you're a pain in my ass, but you already know that." Hank chuckled at her appalled face. "How about I make you a deal. We stay for two hours and if after two hours you still want to kill everyone, we'll leave. On the way home, we'll pick up your favorite ice cream. Sound good?"

Olive couldn't help but side-eye him. "What's in it for you?"

"You sleep in my bed tonight." He looked at her. "The *whole* night."

This caused her to grumble even more. "I get two pints of ice cream and you lock that monster out."

Hank shook his head with a laugh. "Deal."

Olive did her best to ignore his amused face as she pulled out her phone and looked at the time. Two hours, she could do that. She could suck it up for a few hours and in return be rewarded with ice cream and sex. That would be a win-win if you asked her.

She swiped across her screen and opened up her recent text messages.

She maneuvered through her phone pulling up her and Miranda's recent conversation.

Quickly she sent off a message:

He's making me go out to be with people...

Olive wasn't surprised she got a reply within seconds.

It's about damn time someone got you out of the apartment.

Rolling her eyes, Olive sent back her reply:

You don't get it. He's making me go to a cookout with the people at the station. Miranda, you know how I don't do well in crowds.

Why was Miranda such a piece of work?

What crowd? You're going to be surrounded by hot men. I'd kill to be in your shoes right now. Damn, I just wiped drool from my mouth.

Olive shuddered in disgust.

You do know you're gross right?

Dang it, Olive missed her. She was happy Miranda was living her dream, but she couldn't help but feel how her absence affected her.

This is coming from the woman who writes erotic romance...

Narrowing her eyes at her phone she sent her reply.

Sex isn't gross.

Annoyed, Olive was about to put her phone away when another reply came in.

Neither is looking at hot men. Now, make me proud. Go out there mingle with said hot men and if you're lucky you'll get lucky.

If she only knew...

Use this as a research opportunity, Olive. Don't make me come after you!

Olive rolled her eyes. She didn't know about using this as a research opportunity, but she did know one thing. Looking down at her shirt she grinned from ear to ear. She was positive she'd be getting a reaction from Hank's station mates.

Absolutely positive.

Hank pulled into the park with Olive at his side. He still couldn't believe the turn of events that had transpired. The past five days had been his ultimate fantasy come to life. Who would have thought Olive not only would have agreed to move their relationship into a better direction, and in a way that involved him getting to taste every inch of her body any time he wanted? He also still couldn't believe how truly mind-blowing she really was.

Just this morning she jumped him in the shower.

He was one lucky bastard.

Now if he could only make her see he wanted this to be permanent. He wasn't quite sure how to make her understand that, but he'd figure it out. Hank was just glad, his "only them" terms were being met.

If he got word any other man had touched her, hell even looked at her, he'd lose his shit.

His hands clenched the steering wheel with more force.

Then there was her ridiculous, "no one else could know"

clause. Leave it to Olive to still find a way to drive him batshit crazy.

Glancing out of the corner of his eye, he saw her sitting in the seat, her bottom lip between her teeth. The unease he saw in her features made his gut clench.

Shit.

Doing his best to tamper down the lump in his throat he vowed to show her a good time. That was the whole point of bringing her to this cookout. She didn't have to spend her entire life cooped up in the apartment. There was a world of adventure out there for her, she just needed to take a step out the front door. Plus, he liked the idea of being able to show her off in front of his friends.

He reached out his right hand, before placing it on her knee. "Don't look like someone kicked your dog."

She snapped her head toward him. "I'm not."

"Olive, you look like I'm taking you to the death chamber."

"You might as well be."

Hank rolled his eyes before he gave her knee a quick squeeze. He then leaned over and placed a chaste kiss on her cheek.

"What are you doing?" She quickly pulled away.

"Comforting you." He cocked his brow at her.

Olive wiped her cheek. "Not where people could see!"

With a huff, Hank opened his door. "Leave it to you to be a buzz kill."

"I am not a buzz kill. We have rules, mister."

Hank ignored her as he hopped out of the car and jogged over to the passenger side of the vehicle.

When he opened the door, the annoyed looked on Olive's face, made him smirk.

"Don't look at me like that," she grumbled before hopping out of the car.

"Like what?"

"Like you've seen me naked." She cringed. "It creeps me out."

"I have seen you naked."

"I know that and you know that. But the rest of the world doesn't need to know that."

Yes, they do, Hank fought himself to not speak the words out loud. *They all need to know* you're *mine and to back the fuck off.*

Knowing he couldn't say what he wanted, he decided to change directions. "Olive Oil, I'm looking at you like this because I still can't believe you wore that shirt." He watched as she looked down at her top.

When she glanced back at him, the smirk on her face said it all.

"This old thing?" Her eyes gleamed with so much mischief it was hard not to laugh.

"Yes, that old thing." Hank's brows shot up. "You do know the second the guys see you in a "Bigfoot Doesn't Believe in You Either" shirt they are going to be all over you, right?"

Olive shrugged slightly. "Oh, whatever do you mean?"

Her words caused his smile to spread from ear to ear. Olive never ceased to amaze him. Leave it to her to show up wearing a shirt like that to a cookout with a group of men that made it an art form of ragging on people. The wide smile on her face indicating she was ready for battle had him smirking.

Brave girl.

Stupid girl.

But, nonetheless *his* brave stupid girl.

As he scanned her one more time, his heart swelled. That's what she was.

His girl.

Even if she didn't realize it.

"What took you so long?" Lucas yelled from across the park where the grill was set up. "Did you lose your keys again, Tank?"

"I bet it was his cell phone," Rick hollered.

"Nah, he probably lost his wallet!" Tim shouted.

Hank shook his head. "Fuck off." He placed his hand on the small of Olive's back before lightly pushing her toward his friends. "I didn't lose anything." He smirked their way. "I just like to take my time."

"Take your time my ass." Rick laughed, while he flipped a burger on the grill.

Before Hank could respond, Olive's voice broke through the chatter. "Not true, he lost his keys," she announced joyfully ratting him out.

"Is that how you want to play this, Olive Oil?" Hank looked down at Olive, his brow raised.

Olive crossed her arms over her chest. "I don't know what you're talking about."

"That's one."

Her eyes widened. "One what?"

"That's two."

Olive took a step back. "Hold your horses there. What in the world does that even mean?"

Hank matched her movements before blocking her from the view of his buddies. He leaned into her frame before the corners of his mouth turned up. "You know exactly what that means, babe. It's a promise." He raised his right palm showing her his hand.

Olive's mouth fell open before her gaze narrowed on him. "I'll strangle you," she growled.

Hank shrugged. "We can make it three."

"Tank, leave the poor girl alone. No one wants to be crowded by your dumb ass." Lucas laughed before pushing

Hank out of the way. "It's nice to see you again, Olive. How've you been?"

Hank watched as Olive's eyes morphed from anger toward him to joy as she looked at Lucas. "Life could be better." She pointed at Hank. "I have him as a roommate."

Lucas threw his head back as he held his stomach and laughed.

Oh, she was gonna get it. When Olive looked back at him, he mouthed 'four' which caused her lips to thin before turning on her heel to get away from him in a huff.

Damn, he loved her.

Now if only he could get her to realize that.

"Nice shirt," Rick remarked when Olive made her way toward the grill. "Do you believe in Bigfoot?"

As Hank followed behind her, he did his best to hold down the excitement of the show that he knew was about to begin.

Olive placed her hands on her hips ready for a fight.

Oh, this is about to get good.

"Of course, I do." She looked Rick up and down. "Don't you?"

Tim stood next to Rick. "Not on your life, sweet cheeks."

"What he said." Rick pointed at Tim.

When Olive took a step closer to them while puffing her chest out to appear bigger than she really was, it took everything inside of Hank not to fall onto the ground laughing.

"Well, why not?" Olive placed her hands on her hips. "Give me one example of why you think Bigfoot isn't real?"

"If Bigfoot were real we'd have evidence," Rick remarked while Tim nodded his agreement.

"We do have evidence. Haven't you heard of the footprints, the random stray hair that is found, or what about the noises?"

Olive took a small step toward his friends, causing Hank's

gut to clench as he kept in is laughter. *Oh, shit, you can't make this stuff up. I'm gonna break a rib.*

"Where's the body then, sweet cheeks? If there were a Bigfoot around we'd have found its bones by now."

"Exactly," Rick agreed with Tim. "And, might I add if there really were a Bigfoot, I would have shot him already. Plus, I majored in biology in college, so I'd know."

Tim turned toward Rick. "Didn't you used to hunt with your dad? Don't you think you would have seen him if he were real?"

Hank watched as Olive's eyes narrowed. "Bigfoot probably saw you coming and ran the other way. No creature wants to be near stupid."

Hank couldn't hold it in anymore, this time he burst out laughing. He turned to Rick and Tim, with his hand placed on his stomach trying to control his laughter. "I told you she was feisty."

"You need to bring her around more," Lucas said, standing next to Hank as they watch the scene play out. "She'll make our get-togethers a hell of a lot more entertaining."

"Trust me, I know."

Olive turned toward him. "Hank, you believe in Bigfoot, right?"

"Yes, Hank." Rick nodded his head toward him. "Please explain to your girlfriend there is no logical way in hell there is a Bigfoot."

Is this real life? This can't be happening right now? Hank shook his head. He was smarter than to go against the person that was sleeping with him. He shrugged. "Sure, why not," he answered the exact same time Olive yelled, "I'm not his girlfriend."

Olive took a step back from the group, her eyes held the same panic he saw in the SUV when he kissed her.

Tim's face twisted in surprise. "Hank, you really believe in

Bigfoot?"

Hank hadn't really put much thought into it before, but if Olive was adamant there was a big hairy creature roaming the earth, then fine, he'd believe it too. "Why not? You said there isn't any evidence that Bigfoot is real, but there also isn't any evidence that Bigfoot isn't real."

"Hang on," Olive chimed in, throwing her hands in the air. "Can we please go back to the fact I am *not* his girlfriend? I'm his doormat roommate that somehow was forced into coming to this thing."

"You didn't want to hang out with us?" Lucas placed his hand over his chest. "That hurts, doll."

Olive blinked a few times caught off guard. "No." When Lucas raised his brow she tried to backpedal. "It's not that I didn't want to come, I swear. It's just that I don't really like to come to these type of things."

Lucas nodded his head. "So, you didn't want to be here with us. That's what it sounds like you're saying."

Hank watched as Olive struggled. Was it wrong for him to find so much joy in this? Probably.

He knew the guys were ruthless and once they found something to hone in on, it was like open season.

He'd give it another minute before he'd step in.

"Do you think we're not fun?" Tim asked. "You thought we'd be boring, right?"

"Yeah." Rick cocked his head to watch her. "Did you think if you came out with us you'd have a lousy time?"

"No. No, not at all." Olive took another step back before sending Hank a pleading glance.

Show time.

Hank cracked his knuckles before moving to stand beside her. "Of course Olive didn't want to hang out with you numb-nuts. Why would she?"

"Who are you calling a numb-nut?" Rick pointed the

tongs at him.

"Yeah, Tank. Of the three of us, you're the one who would lose your head if it wasn't attached."

"Speaking of that." Lucas turned to face Tim and Rick. "You both owe me twenty bucks."

As the guys started arguing about who owed who money, Hank pulled Olive closer to his side, before he whispered in her ear. "All you have to do is give them something else to bitch about."

Olive's sea blue eyes honed in on him. "Thank you," she whispered.

Hank's face turned into a smirk. "I know exactly how you can thank me." He moved his hand from her lower back to rest on her ass before he squeezed.

"I am not letting you spank me," she growled.

"First, you love it when I spank you," Hank remarked matter-of-fact. "Second, that's not how you're going to thank me from saving you from my dickhole friends."

Olive crossed her arms over her chest. "I do not."

Hank pulled her body closer to his, with his hand still firmly placed on her ass. "I bet you twenty bucks if I bent you over right now, you'd be ready to take me. The thought of me spanking your perfect round ass has you soaking. Don't lie to yourself or me."

Hank heard her breath hitch.

Told you.

"But," he said, drawing her attention to him. "That's not how you're going to thank me."

Her annoyance was back in an instant. "Oh really. Then how?"

Hank spanked her ass lightly before he took off in a jog. When he was a few steps away from her, he looked over his shoulder and smirked. "Tomorrow. Dog has a vet appointment and you just volunteered to take her."

CHAPTER TWELVE

OLIVE STARED at the cat carrier Hank left on the coffee table before he went to the station. She still couldn't fathom how Hank had eventually gotten her to agree to take Dog to the vet. Even when she tried to protest he distracted her with the dang appendage between his legs.

What's a girl to do when that thing comes at you?

Olive shook her thoughts away as she glanced around the room. Of course, Dog was nowhere to be found. Why would she be? That would make things easy.

"Here kitty-kitty."

Olive heard a noise from behind the couch, so she called again. "Here kitty-kitty. Nice kitty, nice freakishly large kitty that is actually the size of a toddler, but Hank still somehow insists you're a cat."

Dog stepped from behind the couch and stared her down.

Holy crap on a stick.

What was she supposed to do now?

Nonchalantly, Olive took a step closer to the cat. "Hey Dog, nice seeing you around," she spoke before pushing the cat carrier closer to the animal.

Dog blinked slowly at her.

Please don't be sizing me up? Please, oh sweet mother of all things chocolate, please. Olive squared her shoulders before she pushed out her chest. "Do you want to go for a car ride? Animals like car rides, right?"

The creature yawned showing its teeth.

"Dog in name only." Olive held her hands in surrender. "Gotcha."

She walked closer to the carrier before she gently pushed it a few inches closer to Dog.

There is only one thing left to do. Olive looked toward the ceiling. *Universe, ole powerful whatever you are, I am begging you please let this run smoothly. I don't want to end up on one of those late-night shows where they tell everyone I was eaten alive by a house cat.*

Olive did her best to take another calming breath. Too bad her hands were shaking. She looked at Dog once more. "Trust me, this is going to hurt me more than it's going to hurt you."

Dog cocked her head to the side and watched as Olive took yet another step closer to her.

One. Two. Three. Jump!

Olive leaped toward Dog. Her arms were out, ready to grab her and wrestle her to the floor if need be.

The she-devil, however, saw Olive's plan coming from a mile away. Dog ran the opposite direction of Olive's propelled body.

Olive landed on the floor with a loud thump. Dog stood a few feet from her, giving her a look that could only be described as "are you serious?".

"Well, that hurt. Why in the hell did I think that was going to work?" Olive blew her hair out of her face. "What is wrong with me?"

A lot.

"Okay, new game plan." Olive pushed herself up before stretching out her body. *Hank better know he owes me a massage after this.* Olive tapped her finger on her chin. "How can you convince an animal to go willingly into a carrier? Especially, one that hates your guts!"

Tuna!

That's precisely how you do it. All cats love tuna, right? *You haven't quite confirmed the creature is a cat though. What if it's only pretending to be a cat. Maybe Dog is some weird alien race that gets offended if you try and feed it tuna?* Olive bit her bottom lip as she contemplated her next move.

She took one look at the carrier and then back at Dog.

Screw it.

Olive ran to the kitchen opening the cupboards looking for the treat to entice Dog into her temporary dungeon.

When Olive found the can, she did a happy dance. "Eureka!" She quickly opened the tuna throwing its contents into a bowl.

With a smug smile on her face and a pat on her back for her pure genius-ness, Olive walked back into the living room. "I'll just place this in the carrier and as soon as Dog walks in I'll shut the gate. Simple as that."

Damn, I'm good. I should be crowned Queen Solver of all Problems!

Too bad Dog had other plans. The moment Olive walked out of the kitchen Dog jumped between her legs causing Olive to lose her footing. The tuna went flying through the air, while Olive tumbled onto the ground landing on her hands and knees.

"Son of a monkey's biscuit!"

Once Olive finally got her bearings on what the hell just transpired she looked up to see Dog eyeing her as she scarfed down the tuna.

"Oh, for the love of all things."

Olive flipped around so she was sitting on her butt. *What the hell am I supposed to do now?*

She took a quick glance at the palms of her hands and her knees. At least the universe had her back there.

No cuts. Check.

Evil she-devil creature staring me down as she eats. Double check.

Could right now get any worse? As Olive decided the world was against her, she fell backward onto the floor with a sigh. "How has my life come to this?"

Oh yeah, that's right. Hank the freakin' Tank.

After a few minutes of her pity party, Olive pushed herself into the seated position. That's when she saw Dog lick her lips one last time as she finished off the tuna before she turned and leisurely walked straight into the carrier.

"What the hell?" Olive's mouth fell open.

As her brain finally registered where Dog was, she jumped toward the carrier slamming the gate shut before locking it in place.

Olive wasn't sure why Dog decided to take pity on her, but she wasn't one to look a gift horse in the mouth. She checked to make sure the gate was securely closed before she placed her hand on her chest, trying to calm her erratic heartbeat.

"Step one. Done."

Olive gathered all her hair before placing it on the top of her head in a bun.

"Now on to step two." As Olive looked at the huge cat carrier which now housed an equally colossal cat she thought about her next options. She wasn't a fan of taking her car anywhere. She couldn't even remember the last time she drove it. It was old and had questionable brakes. She never wanted to chance taking it.

On the rare occasion she had to leave the apartment, she walked.

She took another look at the carrier and she knew she had no other choice but to take the death trap. Realizing her fate, she groaned. Olive then grabbed her keys and phone before searching for the address Hank had given her.

When she was ready Olive walked over to the carrier and heaved with all her might lifting the thing.

"Jesus, what the hell does Hank feed you?"

Olive heard a hiss from inside which had her quickly apologizing. "Sorry, kitty. Nice kitty. My bad kitty."

Let's get this over with.

Fifteen minutes later with the creature in her backseat screaming at the top of its lungs and a few turnover issues with her car Olive finally made it to the building.

Olive opened her phone once more, making sure she was in the correct place. "Richman Veterinarian Hospital. Sounds about right," Olive mumbled before looking into the backseat once more. "All right, she-devil let's get this show on the road."

After another ten minutes, Olive finally managed to get Dog into the clinic.

"Hi ya, there," the curvy receptionist greeted as Olive huffed herself through the door.

"Hi," Olive managed to get out a strangled hello as she did her best to bring her breathing under control. When she made it to the counter, she placed Dog on the floor. "My roommate's cat has an appointment."

The receptionist smiled sweetly, pointing at the clipboard in front of her. "Put your name on the sign in sheet and someone will call you shortly."

Olive nodded.

You mean I'm gonna have to take this thing over to the waiting area? She looked at the carrier again. *I better have bodybuilder arms after this.*

As Olive signed her name, she noticed the receptionist had moved her chair. Her heart melted as she saw a Corgi sleeping on a dog bed. *How cute!*

Much to her surprise, the Corgi opened one of its eyes, before making a small huff as if it was sizing her up.

What the hell? "Is that dog judging me?"

The receptionist turned her chair around to look behind her. "Lord Waffles? Oh, I'm sure of it."

"Lord Waffles?" Olive's brows shot to the ceiling.

"Yeah, I love waffles and as you can tell he thinks highly of himself, hence the 'Lord'." The receptionist looked her way before giving her a warm smile. "Our dogs normally don't come into the office, but Ben's receptionist called in sick so he asked me to fill in." She scrunched her face looking back at the Corgi. "He's in timeout right now, though. If he's here he's normally in the back playing with his sister Ripley. I'm Holly Richman. Ben's wife."

Olive did a quick glance around the room. *Who puts a dog in timeout? Isn't that something you only do with children? Oh, shit on a cracker. Did I walk into an alternate universe when I came in? Are all animals replaced with children now? Oh, God. They are gonna be the rulers of the world, and this one is probably their leader.* Olive stared at the Corgi. *I'm onto you.*

Holly stood moving to a cabinet behind her. "Most of the time he's here, he's good enough. But today he's being a stinker." Once she retrieved the paper she was looking for she bent to pat the Corgi on the head.

"Why is he in timeout?" Olive asked not taking her eyes from the soon to be the leader of the world.

The moment the words were out of her mouth the Corgi stood. He faced her, staring her head on. The judgment was substantial in his eyes.

Great! Now when he overthrows the government I'll be the first to go.

Olive placed her hands up in surrender. "No worries, Pancake. I'm sure whatever you did doesn't warrant being placed in timeout."

At the name "Pancake" the dog shot his nose into the air before falling onto the bed like she'd offended it.

What in the world?

"Oh my God, that was awesome." Holly threw herself into the rolling chair as she laughed. "Don't mind him. He's overly dramatic." When Holly pulled herself back to the computer, she reached for the clipboard. In the process though, she knocked over a mug. "Shit! That's the third one this morning."

Olive's eyes widened. Where the heck was she and what the hell was going on? Plus was this lady all right? Olive did her best not to laugh when Holly started to clean up the spilled coffee, only to have a cup of pens fall over.

Holly threw her hands in the air. "Forget it." She moved back to the Corgi before scooting him over and plopping down next to him. The woman pointed behind her as she scratched the Corgi behind the ears, before pointing past Olive. "Have a seat over there. Ben will be with you shortly."

Deciding to leave well enough alone, Olive heaved the carrier to the waiting area, but not before she took one more glance at the Corgi over her shoulder. *I'm watching you.*

Olive nearly dropped the carrier when the Corgi winked at her.

Holy hell.

She did her best to ignore the new leader of the world and went to the waiting room.

Olive only waited about ten minutes before she was called.

"Dog?"

"That's us." Olive stood readying herself to carry the monster once again. However, the man in a white lab coat beat her to it.

Olive took a step back not sure what to do. The chances of this guy stealing Dog were slim to none.

Oh, how nice it would be if he was stealing Dog, though...

She hadn't been to a vet hospital before, but was this normal?

She followed behind as the man placed the carrier on the exam table like it weighed nothing. "Hank left a message that someone else would be bringing her in," the man spoke.

Olive couldn't take her eyes off him. She didn't know if it was the honey that poured out of his mouth when he spoke or the fact that he took Dog from her so she wouldn't have to carry her, but she could swear she was in love with this man.

Dumb dumb, he's married and you have Hank. She blanched. *I do not have Hank,* she argued with herself. *We are doing the nasty and it's purely for research.* She looked at the man again. Looking wasn't against the law, plus, she was always storing away information in her head for future characters.

The man cocked his head to the side regarding her. "I'm Dr. Ben Richman." He held out his hand to her.

"Olive." She took his outreached hand.

"It's nice to meet you."

Olive nodded. "Ditto."

The doctor chuckled before he reached for the carrier gate. "Let's get this show on the road."

Thirty disastrous minutes later, Olive walked out of the clinic.

She still couldn't wrap her mind fully around what had happened. The moment the doctor opened the gate Dog took off like a bat out of hell.

Dog was on a mission and that mission was to get the hell

out of there, and she didn't care about the number of casualties she left in her wake. To her, the more the merrier.

Olive had to jump on top of the bench in the room to avoid Dog trying to kill her. Too bad her attempt to save herself was short-lived.

As the doctor and vet tech ran around the room trying to capture the monster, it turned out, Olive's left leg had been a perfect target for Dog.

Olive saw her whole life flash before her eyes.

As the cat jumped to seek her revenge and finally do Olive in, Dr. Richman had intercepted the creature. Once she was under control, Dog got her shots and was shoved back in the carrier.

There was no way in hell she was *ever* bringing that thing back here. No amount of sexy times would change her mind.

Finally, Olive placed Dog in her backseat. She got into the driver's side before she plopped her head onto the steering wheel.

"Well, that was fun."

Dog answered her with a meow, then a hiss.

Olive's eyes narrowed as she turned to face the creature. "Oh, I bet it was loads of fun for you." She was about to start the car when her phone rang. When Olive saw the picture of a shirtless Hank, she rolled her eyes. Leave it to him to make his caller ID be a shirtless photo of him. Albeit, it was a sexy photo.

She bit her bottom lip lightly, knowing exactly what was only a few inches lower that the picture had cut off.

Olive shook the thoughts out of her head. She was mad at him, and that's how she planned to stay for the time being. "Yes," she answered.

"How was Dog?" Hank's deep voice came through the line causing her body to involuntary shiver.

Get it together body! Now is not the time. "She was a pain in the ass, Hank. How else do you think that would have gone?" She looked in her rearview mirror to see Dog staring at her, before licking her lips. *Jesus.*

Olive heard Hank chuckle. "*I'm sure she was fine. Did she get all of her shots? Did she get a clean bill of health?*"

She rolled her eyes. "Only after she decided to take a lunge at my leg and Doctor Richman was able to catch her in the air, yes, she got her shots. And, a clean bill of health. If you want to call an unnatural desire for spilled blood healthy, that is."

"*That's good to hear.*" Hank clearly ignored her. "*I'll be home early tonight. I traded with one of the guys on first shift.*"

Olive's face hardened as his words registered. "Wait a freakin' minute there, Bub? Hank, are you telling me you purposely traded to have an early shift so *I* would have to take the creature to the vet?" She was going to kill him.

When Olive heard Hank burst into laughter over the phone, she lost it. "I swear to all things sugary and delicious, Hank, the moment I get my hands on you, you're gonna regret it. When you mess with me, you lose every time. Remember that."

Olive thought he'd disconnected the phone when she didn't hear a reply. However, after a few deafening moments, Hank's voice broke through the silence. "*That's where you're wrong, Olive Oil. I win the second you get your hands on me.*"

CHAPTER THIRTEEN

Three Months Later

OLIVE WAS SPRAWLED out on her bed, with Hank right beside her. It had been an interesting few months, to say the least, but Olive wasn't complaining. Not when she got to spend her nights, shower time, and random intervals throughout the day at the mercy of Hank's body.

Overall, her writing had improved too. Olive no longer found herself writing thousands of useless words, or staring at a blank page for hours. Her sexy times scenes also improved. Instead of constantly scolding herself for daydreaming about Hank's body, she let it flow and wrote everything she thought about down. She was back to her original writing self.

She had Hank to thank for that.

Even if she didn't want to admit it.

Olive felt the bed dip at her feet.

"Here she comes," Hank's groggy voice sounded from next to her.

Olive looked at the end of the bed to see that Dog had indeed decided to grace them with her presence. Over the past few months, even her relationship with Dog had improved tremendously.

Well, sort of.

Most of the time they tolerated each other, which was an improvement from when Dog was trying to eat her.

"Here kitty," Olive said, patting her thigh.

"You know she doesn't like that," Hank announced before pushing himself up to lay his back against the headboard. "It's Dog or nothing. She takes offense to *kitty*."

Olive crossed her arms over her naked chest. "For your information, she lets me call her kitty."

Hank turned to her, his eyes narrow. "No, she lets you live because you've taken to feeding her tuna when I'm not looking."

The fake menace in his voice had Olive shrugging. "Toe-ma-toe. Ta-ma-toe. Same thing."

"Whatever you say, Olive Oil." Hank grabbed her waist and hoisted her onto his lap.

"Hey!" she screamed before she fixed herself so she was more comfortably situated on him. "No manhandling."

"You like it when my man hands handle you." To emphasize his point, he started moving his hands up her curves until he reached her shoulders. He then placed one of his hands behind her neck bringing her to him.

"Whatever." Olive leaned into his touch as he moved closer. He placed his head in the crook of her neck.

"I don't want to get out of bed yet," Hank grumbled as he started kissing down her throat.

Olive instantly moved her head to the side giving him better access. "We don't ever have to get out. As long as you keep doing what you're doing, we can stay here forever for all I care."

Hank pulled away causing Olive to nearly fall into him as her skin still begged for his touch.

"I have work in a few hours and you need to start that next book," the bastard said.

She wanted to punch the smug look right off his face. "Who died and made you my boss?"

Hank spanked her ass causing her to jump. "You love it when I'm the boss."

True.

"I just let you believe you're the boss." Olive jutted her chin out in defiance, but lost the battle when Hank leaned forward lightly biting it.

"Is that so?" In one move, Hank flipped her before pinning her body beneath him. *Yes, please.* Her body opened for him. There was something about letting Hank take control of her that drove her body to obey him instantly.

As Hank had her arms pinned above her head, he started peppering kisses down her body causing her to laugh. However, her laughter was short-lived when he reached her left breast.

Hank let his tongue circle her nipple before he drew it into his mouth. Olive's body arched into his mouth, begging.

"More," she moaned. "Give me all you've got, Captain."

Hank released her with a pop before he looked at her. "Really?" He cocked his right brow.

Why is it whenever he does that, it's so sexy?

"Less talkie more suckie," she demanded as she ignored the amusement in his eyes.

Hank shook his head with a chuckle before he moved his mouth back to her nipple. He then moved her hands so he could pin her down with only one of his hands. The other started to migrate down her body. He let his fingers move across her curves.

The moment his hand reached her stomach her first reaction was to tense. However, the gentle caress she felt on her skin from Hank reminded her he'd already seen every inch of her body. And not once had he complained, on the contrary, he worshipped every lump, bump, and stretch mark she had.

Olive hadn't known when her insecurities changed around Hank, but they had. Instead of rushing to hide under the covers, she freely walked around naked.

Hank made her forget her imperfections.

Olive worked her bottom lip trying to make sense of the newfound knowledge.

However, the second Hank's hand reached her mound all thoughts were lost. Her eyes rolled back into her head as his fingers stroked her.

"That's right, baby," Hank's voice broke through her trance. "Let go." He sought out her clit causing her body to jerk at the sensation.

"More, please more," Olive pleaded as she felt herself teeter on the edge.

"I'll give you more." Hank removed his hand from Olive's core, causing her to jerk forward.

I'll kill him!

Frustration coursed through her body. "That is not more," she growled. "That's *less.* Do you need me to *Google* it for you?" She tried to release her hands from his hold but couldn't fight him off.

"Oh, you do know how I love it when feisty Olive comes out and plays," he said before he took both of his hands to pin her once more. Hank used his knees to open her, before using his hips to guide his dick to her entrance. "You wanted more, Olive. Is that right?"

Her lips thinned as her eyes narrowed. "You better be glad you're holding my hands right now or I'd punch you right in the jaw. Now stop dilly-dallying and fuck me." She pushed her hips to his trying to get him to enter her, but had no luck. He pulled back right as she tried.

"What my Olive wants, my Olive gets." He thrust himself forward entering her with ease.

Poking the beast is fun, her thoughts ran through her head.

She knew damn well what she was doing.

"That's all you got?" Olive yelled as he switched his movements making sure to hit her spot with each thrust.

"Oh, now you are gonna get it."

Yes, please!

Hank pulled Olive's body closer as they both collapsed onto the bed. She always molded perfectly to him.

He took a quick glance at the clock on Olive's nightstand. Thankfully, he still had a few hours before he needed to get ready for work. Right now, all he wanted to do was infuse Olive into his skin and never let go.

He still couldn't fathom how everything had played out between them. The fact he was in her bed right now, made him want to jump in the air. Sure, they still got into some knock down drag out fights, but Hank was almost positive Olive did them on purpose.

He knew he did.

Make-up sex was the best.

He pulled her even closer to his body before he rested his head on top of hers.

Nothing could get better than this.

Hank tightened his hold on Olive. He couldn't help but smile when he saw the Christmas tree in the corner.

He cast his eyes down to watch her. Olive's face glowed perfectly as the twinkling lights bounced off her features. "You never told me why you insist on having a Christmas tree up all year."

Hank felt Olive squirm in his arms before getting comfortable once again. "I just do."

"That's not an answer, Olive."

Moving a little, she shrugged. "It's weird. And you'll think

I'm strange or some crazy person."

"I kinda already do." He laughed when she elbowed him. "I'm kidding, you know I don't *kinda* already do. I know one hundred percent you're weird. Hit me with all your weirdness." At this point, there was nothing that would surprise him anymore.

Olive laughed before she huffed out a sigh. "Fine. You know how it was with my parents growing up, right?"

"Yeah," he growled. "Don't remind me." His hand that was on her stomach instinctively squeezed protectively pulling her closer.

"Down killer." She laughed. "Anyway, it might sound silly, but during the holidays it was different. Maybe it was all the parties my parents would throw, or whatever. But when the Christmas tree came out, it was like I was free. I was no longer their disappointment of the family. Instead, I was just there. I could go on living my day to day life without fear of their judgment."

"Olive..." His heart clenched.

"I think they were always too busy making themselves look better during that time to realize I was even there."

His heart broke for her.

"In a weird way, the holidays were my happiest time. Each year I knew the second I saw the tree, I could breathe a sigh of relief if only for a few weeks. As the years went on, I found my holiday spirit more and more. Do you remember the year Miranda and I threw powdered sugar all over your living room so we could make snow angels?"

Hank huffed out a laugh at the memory. "I do, baby. My mom was pissed."

Olive turned her face toward him. The corners of her mouth turned up in a mischievous smile. "For all of five minutes before she got onto the floor and did them with us."

Hank laughed before he placed a swift kiss on the top of

her forehead. His parents were such a contrast to hers. Where Olive's parents were cold and unforgiving, his were warm and welcomed everyone with open arms.

He couldn't wait to finally be able to tell his mom, Olive was his girl. He knew both his parents would be over the moon about it.

There was only one thing stopping him.

He needed Olive to see it too.

"The Christmas tree also reminds me to be a realist."

Hank cocked his head to the side as he studied her.

"I watched from the sidelines how my parents acted. They were always at each other's throats. They'd fight about anything and everything. From their silverware set, to their napkin pattern. Who was popular enough to be invited to their parties and so on. I'd lay under the tree with a book in my hand and watch as they argued with each other. As soon as a guest would arrive, they'd be the doting couple, it was nauseating."

"I'm sorry, Olive."

"Why are you sorry?"

"I hate you had to grow up like that." Hank looked at the ceiling fan. "No wonder you were always at our house."

"Your house was better."

He looked back at Olive. "I used to pick on you because I never understood why you'd willingly spend all your time with us when you had one of the biggest houses in the area. I used to envy what it would be like to grow up being the rich kid."

Olive jerked out of his grasp to stare at him. "I was never the rich kid."

"I didn't know that. At the time I picked on you because I wanted what you had. I never understood why you were always around when you had something better at home, or at least I thought you did. I didn't really know how bad it was. I used to call you names and mess with yours and Miranda's stuff because I was jealous. Then when you got older I found myself attracted to you, so I continued with the constant teasing."

Olive's eyes softened when she looked at him. "It could have been worse. I had a roof over my head and Lord knows enough food. It wasn't all that bad."

"And yet you have a Christmas tree in your room."

"The Christmas tree keeps me free." When Olive looked at the tree he saw awe in her eyes. "It reminds me that I can be who I want to be. I'll never take it down."

Hank realized what the tree meant to her.

Freedom.

At that moment he finally understood who Olive was. As she watched her tree and took in what it represented to her, he found himself falling more in love with her.

It was like he was seeing her for the first time.

"I'm in love with you, Olive Quinn." The words were out of his mouth before his brain processed what he was doing. However, now that the words were out there, he wasn't going to take them back. He didn't care. He wanted her to know he loved her.

Olive flinched away from him. "What did you say?"

"You heard me. I love you." His eyebrows knitted together.

"No, you don't." Olive moved off the bed reaching for her pants that had been discarded the previous night. "You're mistaken. You're on some post-sex high or something like that."

Hank pushed himself off the bed following her as she moved around her room getting dressed. "These aren't words thrown out in the heat of the moment. You can't tell me how I feel, Olive. I know for a fact I'm in love with you."

"You are not in love with me, Hank."

"Yeah, I am." Hank bent picking up his pants before

hastily throwing them on. "I've been in love with you for as long as I can remember."

Olive stopped getting dressed and stared at him. Her eyes held fear. "Why are you lying?"

Hank pulled on his shirt. "I'm not fucking lying, Olive."

"You already get in my pants. You don't need to butter me up to *keep* getting into my pants. I'm a sure thing when it comes to you. You don't need to lie to keep me here."

"You have got to be kidding me right now." Hank felt his body was on the verge of snapping.

"I'm not the one that's kidding you. You're kidding yourself if you think you're in love with me."

Hank's eyes narrowed on her as she finished putting on her top.

"I'm sure by the time you come home from the station, this will have all blown over and we can get to the make-up sex part and forget this ever happened."

Hank shook his head in anger before he left her room. Olive was right behind him. When they made it into the living room, Hank quickly threw on his boots. He needed to get out of there.

"This isn't like normal fights, Olive. This is me telling you I'm in love with you and I'm so fucking tired of you pretending my feelings don't count. What more do you want me to do?"

Olive crossed her arms over her chest as she stared him down. "You don't love me, Hank. It's not possible."

"Yes, I do. I've been in love with you for years. Fucking years, Olive. Did you really think I needed to move in here?"

He watched as her eyes widened. "Because, I didn't. The second Miranda told me you needed a new roommate I jumped at the chance."

Olive threw her chin out. "Why?"

"Jesus Olive, are you not fucking listening? I love you. I

am in love with you and I want to spend the rest of my goddamn life with you." Hank straightened before taking a small step closer to her.

When she took a step away from him...

His heart sank.

"This was only supposed to be research, Hank."

Her words were like a knife to his chest. He stared at her with pure disbelief in his eyes.

"Is that what you really think these last few months have been?" He made air quotes. "*Research?*"

"Yes." She blinked at him. "That-that's what you said this was. That's why I agreed to do it. You can't change the rules now. Hank that's not the agreement."

Hank looked into her eyes hoping he'd see something that would make him stay. Something that would tell him he had a chance of changing her mind.

Instead, he saw her raise her walls around herself.

Shaking his head, he grabbed his keys and headed toward the door and pulled it open. He turned to look at her one more time. "You got what you want, Olive. I'm un-agreeing to whatever it was we had. I can't do this anymore. Fuck, I won't do this anymore. Consider us done. If all I am to you is research then you need to find yourself another subject because I can't keep loving you if you refuse to love me too."

CHAPTER FOURTEEN

OLIVE JUMPED the moment Hank slammed the door behind him. As she looked around the room she tried to grasp what had just happened. How did she go from being in bed with Hank to this?

"Oh yeah, that's right. Hank told me he loved me."

Olive plopped onto the couch trying to analyze everything as she always did.

Hank doesn't love me. He can't love me.

Olive's body pulled into itself. Was whatever they had really over? Was this the end of their agreement?

At that thought, her heart constricted in pain.

No. This isn't supposed to hurt. This isn't supposed to be anything.

Olive looked around the room. When she spotted Dog, she realized the cat was intently staring at her. She could swear she saw shame in Dog's eyes.

"Stop looking at me like that," Olive pleaded. "He can't love me, Dog. There are so many reasons why he can't be in love with me. I'm not his type, for one."

Dog threw her head into the air as if to tell her she was wrong.

"I'm right. Hank Parker is known for loving and leaving them. Plus, he's my best friend's brother. There are so many things wrong with this fucked up agreement."

Olive threw herself backward onto the couch as she tried to piece together the events of the morning. This was why she never wanted to do a "friends with benefits" type of relationship. They always caused problems. Even in her books they threw everyone's life upside down.

Although, the characters in her books always seemed to work it out...

Olive squeezed her eyes shut.

Hank wasn't like her characters, though.

He was better.

Hank was perfect.

When it came to Hank, Olive's needs always came first. And he always went above and beyond when taking care of her.

Once Olive had finally gotten her writing groove back, Hank did everything he could to help her.

She thought back to the first time she actually realized Hank had been making sure she was fed and had something to drink during her monster writing sessions.

She hadn't truly registered what he was doing until her stomach grumbled and she mindlessly reached for the ham sandwich he left at her side.

Hank had taken it upon himself to make sure she always had what she needed.

He constantly made sure she had something to drink, a snack, sometimes a full-blown meal. He'd even go as far as to make sure Dog was out of the room.

Since Hank and Olive had started their research agreement, her life had run more smoothly. Everything had run more smoothly. She'd been able to knock out another book well before her deadline. She found herself having more time to read. Life had become less stressful.

But, it wasn't just how he took care of her. It was everything.

She placed the palms of her hands over her closed eyes as she thought of Hank's declaration. Could he really love her?

More importantly, she thought. *Could I love him?*

Olive spent the better part of her life believing love was a lie. She wrote about love and made sure to give every character their deserved happy ending, but she never thought love was in the cards for her.

At least not anymore.

She thought she'd been in love with Josh.

She was wrong.

All Josh did was teach her love was a made-up falsehood. Just like her parents did.

Love wasn't real.

Love was made up, she knew that firsthand since her career involved manipulating her stories so her characters got their happy ending.

What was love anyway?

The only examples she'd been shown her whole life were utter crap. The way her parents treated each other. That wasn't love.

Olive pinched the bridge of her nose as she laid on the couch.

Hank's parents weren't like that, though.

She opened her eyes to stare at the ceiling. That's right. Hank's parents were the complete opposite of hers. When they looked at each other, it was like everyone else in the room melted away.

She'd be lying if she said she didn't want that for herself. Or at least had dreamed about it, back before she wisened up about life.

A small tear ran down the side of Olive's cheek. *I don't deserve love like that.* She closed her eyes as her father's voice rang through her head. *"You are such a failure, Olive. Do you really think anyone would want to be with someone who is an English Literature major? No wonder Josh slept around on you. I'm not surprised in the least. What does surprise me is the fact he was with you in the first place."*

Olive felt more tears break free as her mother's words also chimed in. *"I wish you weren't my daughter."*

Olive pushed away her tears, before she sat upright on the couch. Her parents had beat it into her daily that she wasn't good enough. She wasn't pretty enough. She was too overweight.

She didn't deserve love.

How was Olive supposed to know what love felt like?

She'd never been loved.

Olive closed her eyes while she took a deep breath.

Hank said he loved her.

He was always there for her. He took care of her needs. Needs she didn't even know she had. When she was with him she felt safe, secure, and warmth. A warmth she never felt with her parents.

Could she put aside her warped feelings of love, and see Hank for who he really was?

Her other half.

Olive's eyes shot open at the realization.

Hank was her other half.

The person that completed her in every way possible. It didn't matter her parents warped what love was to her. Because Hank showed her.

Hank showed her every day what it felt like to be loved and cared for, and more importantly, he showed her it was okay to love someone.

Olive Quinn was in love with Hank Parker.

She jumped to her feet. "I have to tell him."

A new wave of urgency ran through her as she scanned the room looking for her keys. When she spotted the keys on the other end of the coffee table, she jumped for them.

However, the second her fingers touched the key ring her body shuddered.

She'd been meaning to take her car in and get it looked at, but she kept putting it off. And the few times she needed to go somewhere that was too far to walk, Hank always offered to drive her.

Olive thought about her options as she bit her bottom lip. *Stop dilly-dallying, girl. You don't have time for this.*

This was too important to wait. Not when the last thing Hank said was they were over.

She couldn't chance it. She was in love with Hank, and if that meant getting into her piece of shit car to drive to the station to tell him, then so be it.

Even if Olive had to tie him to the bed to get him to understand she was also in love with him, she would. She'd gladly do it.

Without a second thought, she grabbed the keys along with her purse and took off toward her car. She was on a mission and nothing was going to stop her.

When she made it outside, she threw open the driver's side door of the car and jumped in. Her hands shook as she placed her keys in the ignition and turned.

Nothing.

"No!" she cried. Olive tried again.

Nothing.

She threw her hands into the air. "Please start, please freakin' start." Olive banged on the steering wheel, her frustrations causing her to snap. She took a deep breath closing her eyes before turning the key one more time.

When her car roared to life, she felt relief flood through

her body. She looked up, giving a silent thank you to the Universe.

With her car started she was back on track.

Olive threw her car into reverse before she pulled out.

Hank was her world and she was going to stop at nothing to tell him.

As she sped down the road her mind remained focused on one thing. Too bad she never saw the other car who'd run the red light coming until it was too late. With her faulty brakes, she didn't stand a chance at stopping in time.

That's when Olive's world turned to black.

CHAPTER FIFTEEN

HANK STORMED INTO THE STATION. His emotions were all over the place, he didn't know whether he wanted to punch a wall or run back to Olive.

He was hurt. He was angry. And, he didn't know where to go from here.

How could Olive not believe in his feelings, was she really that scared? He fucking knew deep down Olive loved him too. There was no way she didn't. She proved it to him every day. The nights she wasn't writing she'd make sure he had a warm meal to come home to. She'd always curl up on the couch with him, and hand him the remote while she read or worked on her stories. She made it a point, subconsciously or not, to be near him.

Even at night, her body would seek his out while she was deep in sleep. She'd wrap herself around him, molding her body to his.

They were the perfect pair. All of their actions were done out of love. Unfortunately, with Olive's fucked up parents warping what love truly was, she didn't know it.

She couldn't see that they were perfect for each other.

And now in the heat of the moment, he'd ended them.

This was only research. His fists clenched. This was not only fucking research, he knew it and she knew it.

"Why do you look liked you are about to kill someone?" Lucas asked, as Hank stormed past him before throwing himself into one of the chairs in the station's kitchen.

"I don't."

"Tank, if you could see yourself right now you'd even stay clear of you."

Hank's jaw firmed as he watched Lucas pour two cups of coffee. The silence in the room was deafening.

"What's got you shootin' daggers out your eyes?" Lucas moved to sit opposite of Hank, pushing the freshly poured coffee in his direction.

"Nothing." Hank grabbed the drink before taking a hefty gulp. A sigh of irritation escaped him when he looked over the rim to see Lucas studying him.

When he started tapping his fingers on the table, Hank clenched his jaw. He knew Lucas was trying to get a rise of out him, but right now was not the time.

After a few minutes, Hank snapped. "Do you mind?"

"Not at all." Lucas brought his mug to his lips to hide a huge grin that Hank was sure he was sporting. Hank's eyes narrowed when Lucas placed the cup back on the table and started to strum his fingers once again.

Hank's eye began to twitch as he watched the hand ready to break it in two. "If you're going to be annoying go be annoying somewhere else," he spat.

Lucas relaxed farther into his chair. "I'm not being any more annoying than I normally am."

Does he have a death wish? Hank held his coffee mug with a force he was sure would shatter it in seconds, as he glared at his friend.

"What? I'm not." Lucas took another drink. "I'm just sittin' here, waitin' for you to tell me what's got your panties in a twist."

"Fuck off!"

"Maybe later." Lucas stared at him giving him the once-over. "I can guess if that'll make it easier on ya?"

Why the fuck is he always like this? Annoying as shit.

Hank pushed himself back into his chair, daring his friend. "Have at it."

"It's either Dog's giving you the cold shoulder again, or you've fucked it up with Olive."

Hank's eyes widened in surprise. "What makes you say that?"

"Are you going to lie to me and tell me it's not?" Lucas moved closer to the table, daring Hank to challenge him.

Hank mimicked Lucas's posture. "No, I'm not denying anything. I was just curious as to why you would say anything had to do with Olive in the first place."

Lucas quirked his brow. "Do you really think I don't know about your relationship with her? I'm your best friend. I've been there all along, I was there at the graduation. I saw the way you looked at her. You've been dreaming about Olive for years."

Hank nodded, but refused to say anything.

"You're sleeping with her."

That got his attention. "How do you know that?"

Lucas shook his head while a small chuckle escaped him. "The cookout was a dead giveaway, man. All the subtle touching and the eye fucking when you thought no one was looking. You were disgustingly protective of her." Lucas leaned back. "You shielded her body from us when we were giving her a hard time. It was nauseating."

Had it been that obvious? Good. Hank wanted to pat himself on the back. Everyone damn well needed to know she belonged to him.

"The guys and I have a bet going on when you'll fuck it up." Lucas pulled out his phone. "Looks like Tim won."

Fuckers!

"I didn't fuck it up," Hank protested.

"From where I'm sitting, it looks like you fucked it up to me."

Hank glared at him, his anger rising. "I told her I love her."

"Yup, you fucked it up." Lucas gave a quick nod before he took another drink of his coffee.

"How can telling her I love her, be the thing that makes me fuck it up?" Hank looked around the room as one of Olive's biggest quirks somehow invaded his mind. Was he now in some weird parallel universe like the ones she'd wax poetic about when she got onto one of her tangents? *Fuck!* Even pissed at her, she was still so far under his skin, he'd even started thinking like her. His jaw firmed. "You don't fuck things up when you tell a woman you are in love with them. That makes zero sense."

"Does it?" Lucas remarked. "Hank, this is Olive we are talking about. The shy girl that would do anything in the world to avoid people. Do you really think she'd be okay with you shouting out I love you? And I bet your dumb ass did it in the middle of boinking her. There is no way in hell she would believe you. So, in turn, you fucked it up."

"I didn't do it in the middle of *boinking* her."

"Really?" Lucas looked impressed.

"It was after."

"Yup, you fucked it up."

Hank's lips flattened as he glared at Lucas.

"Olive is one of those special girls, Tank. You should know better than to have said it like that."

"Well, I did," he snapped. "Then she pretty much told me to fuck off. I fucking saw red, man. It was like I was talking to the wall. She wouldn't listen to reason no matter what I said." Something inside of him broke. "I stormed out of there telling her we were done." As he recalled the shock on her face, his gut clenched. This was never supposed to be like this. When he told her he loved her, she should have jumped into his arms and told him she loved him too.

"So that's that, then?" Lucas asked.

With a solemn nod, Hank answered. "I'm her research subject."

Lucas' brows shot to the ceiling. "Wait, hold up a second. What do you mean *research* subject?"

Hank quickly jumped to Olive's defense. "It's not what you think. She writes those sexy books that women read. I only found out when I happened upon it by accident. To make a long story short, I convinced her to use me as her live-in research subject for the scenes in her books."

"I bet that's been working out for you."

Hank smiled as he waggled his brows before the realization of the morning set back in. "It never was working out for me," he answered honestly. "We fell into this stupid agreement when I've always wanted more. I've wanted more for years, but I was willing to take whatever she gave me."

"And now she won't give you anything."

"That's the kicker. She's willing to keep using my body, but she won't give me her heart." Hank's eyes pleaded with his friend. "I can't do that anymore, Luke. I won't do that anymore. She needs to realize that love is a real thing, what we have is love. I mean for fuck's sake she writes about it."

Lucas moved closer to the table as he pondered the predicament. "Why do you think she writes about it but doesn't believe in it?

"Her parents are all sorts of fucked up."

"Aren't most?"

"If you only knew. They really did a number on her. Hell, man, they still do."

They were both quiet for a few moments before Lucas spoke. "Are you saying you're giving up?"

Hank sat back in his chair. No, he wasn't done. There was no way in hell he was done. Olive was his other half and he was going to stop at nothing to prove it to her. He only said they were over in the heat of the moment. He might be pissed, but he wasn't giving up.

Hank opened his mouth to tell Lucas that, when the alarm rang through the station causing both men to jump to their feet.

Within seconds, both men were back in action.

It only took a few minutes before everyone was in their turnout gear and in the truck headed to a scene of a potentially fatal car crash.

Lucas drove the rig while Hank sat in the passenger seat. The rest of the team was in the back, while Rick and Tim were in the ambulance directly behind them.

Hank did his best to put his situation with Olive out of his mind as he readied himself to get to work. This is what he loved about his job. He thrived on the adrenaline of the unknown.

When he glanced to his left he saw Lucas staring at him. The pity that quickly glanced through his expression before turning back to the road had Hank's body tense.

Now was not the time.

Right now, they had a job to do and as soon as that job was done, he was going to her and they were getting back on track.

As they rounded the corner to the accident he readied himself for whatever was to come.

The moment the accident came into view, Hank's heart stopped.

It can't be!

His face paled as he felt sweat break through his skin. *Please, God no.*

When they pulled to a stop his greatest fears were confirmed. "That's Olive's car!"

Everything came to a screeching halt for Hank.

There in front of him were two mangled cars. Olive's was flipped over with zero signs of movement. Hank bolted out of the rig, protocol be damned.

He propelled his body as fast as he could to Olive's car. When he was a few feet away he skidded on his knees to the crushed driver's side as he screamed her name. "Olive! Olive are you okay? Baby, please answer me!"

He fell to his stomach, crawling through the broken glass and debris trying his best to get to her. When Olive came into view, a new wave of panic rushed through him. Her body hung limply upside down, with blood pouring from her head. He frantically worked his way to her as his mind thought the worst.

"Is it Olive?"

Hank heard the faint words from behind him but didn't bother to acknowledge them. The amount of blood coming from Olive's body horrified him.

"Go check on the other vehicle," Lucas hollered to the others before he fell to his knees next to Hank. "I need you to stay calm, Tank. Right now, you freaking out isn't going to do Olive any favors."

Ignoring him, Hank tried pushing his body through the crushed opening of Olive's window. "I'm in love with her, you don't get it." Hank couldn't get his body to move right. No matter how many times he adjusted his frame he could only reach her limp hand that had fallen into a pool of her blood.

"I know you are, buddy." Lucas took off his glove after pushing Hank out of the way.

Hank watched in horror as Lucas reached for Olive. When he placed his fingers on her neck he heard him breathe a subtle sign of relief. "She's got a pulse. It's faint, but it's there."

Hank let out a breath he hadn't known he'd been holding.

"Hank, man. I know this is rough but I need you to move out of the way so we can get Rick in here."

Hank knew Rick stepping in was the best course of action, but he couldn't find the strength to move away from Olive.

There was so much blood.

Rick pushed his way between him and Lucas. "I'll take good care of her, Hank, I'll die before she does."

At Rick's words, Hank finally let go of Olive's hand and moved away. Once he was back on his feet he stood there in shock as he watched Rick and Lucas work on her.

Tim called from the second vehicle. "Victim is D.O.A."

Hank spun toward Tim and started sprinting his way. "Fuck!" When he got to Tim, he was able to confirm what he'd announced. "Damnit!" Hank punched the side of the car as hard as he could.

This was his worst case scenario come to life.

Looking back at Olive's flipped car he didn't know what else to do. Tim had run to Olive's side as the rest of his team used the Jaws of Life to rip open her car.

He knew between Rick and now Tim they would do everything in their power to keep Olive stable enough to transport her to the hospital.

He couldn't stop his life with Olive from flashing before his eyes. The look she gave him after he told her they were done haunted him.

"Grab the stretcher!"

Hank rushed to the ambulance helping his teammates. While one of them pulled the stretcher out of the back, he yanked the backboard and a collar from the bus and sprinted back to the mangled car.

Within seconds Olive was freed. They placed her on the backboard before getting her onto the stretcher. Hank stayed at her side while Tim checked her eyes for any sign of movement.

"We need to intubate." Hank's stomach sank as they pushed her to the bus. "She's stopped breathing."

"Let's go!" Rick yelled as he ran toward the driver's side door.

Hank turned toward Lucas. "I'm going with her!" He didn't wait for his answer as he hopped into the back of the bus with Tim.

"I wouldn't expect anything less," Lucas hollered back. "I'll meet you at the hospital."

Tim pounded on the back window signaling for Rick to gun it. "We've got to go!"

Hank looked at Olive on the stretcher, her face bloodied and bruised. As he watched Tim work he did his best to assist with her breathing once Tim got her intubated. He'd done his stint with the EMT side of the department just like every other firefighter. But for the life of him, he couldn't keep his mind focused on what to do next.

Not while the love of his life was dying in front of him. "I'm here. Olive, baby. I'm here. Don't you fucking leave me!" He held onto her hand, as tears formed in his eyes. For the first time in years, he prayed. He prayed to see her sea blue eyes just one more time.

"Shit." Tim moved around the back of the ambulance doing everything he could for her.

As Hank watched her blood riddled face, tears poured down his cheeks. "Baby, I need you. Please. Please."

Tim called to Rick. "Put a move on. It's not looking good. I'm losing her." Tim reached for epinephrine.

Hank watched in horror as Olive's eyes opened for a split second before her whole body sagged. That's when she flatlined.

CHAPTER SIXTEEN

EVERYTHING HAD STARTED to look the same as Hank continued to pace throughout the surgical waiting room. Hank rubbed the back of his neck as he mindlessly moved through the confines of the walls, begging for anyone to let him know how Olive was doing.

It'd been hours since Olive had been rushed into surgery, and he hadn't heard anything since.

The door to the surgical ward beeped which caused Hank to freeze in his tracks as he looked toward the door.

Please, be for Olive.

The moment the person made it through the opening and turned away from him, making their way down the hall, his heart fell.

He didn't know how much longer he could take this.

Hank's hands fisted at his side, as he scrunched his eyes closed.

He'd never get the image of Olive's heart stopping in the back of the ambulance out of his head. There had never been a moment he'd been more terrified in his life.

He owed everything he had to Tim. If it weren't for him, Olive wouldn't have made it to the hospital.

Hank opened his eyes only to look down at his blood-soaked uniform. His knees weakened.

Knowing he couldn't stand anymore, he moved over to a nearby chair and collapsed in it. His body hunched over as he placed his head in his hands.

This can't be happening. Not Olive. Not my Olive.

The sight of her blood made bile rise in his throat.

"Have you heard anything?"

Hank looked up to see Lucas make his way into the room with two cups of coffee in his hands.

"Not a damn thing," he answered, as he looked at his watch. "It's been six hours, Luke. Six fuckin' hours." He took the coffee Lucas handed him, with a sigh. *Six hours.*

Lucas' eyebrows drew together before he fell into the seat next to Hank's. "You'd think you would have heard something by now." He pulled out his phone. "Tim text me while I was in the cafeteria. They want to stop by after their shift."

"They don't need to." Hank shook his head in disbelief. "At this point, we don't know how much longer she's gonna be in surgery, or if she'll even make it."

"Don't talk like that, Tank."

"Talk like what? The truth?" With a solemn expression, Hank fell back into his seat. "No one is telling me anything, man. At this point, I don't know what to do or what else to think." Hank looked at his friend, a pained expression marring his face. "I can't lose her, Lucas."

"You won't," he replied before he gripped Hank's shoulder jutting his chin toward the receptionist. "When was the last time you asked for any updates?"

"Five minutes after you left to grab something to eat." Hank shrugged.

He knew he couldn't go back to the receptionist so soon.

At this point, he was sure she was going to call security on him. Every time he passed by the desk, she'd eye him warily, ready to make her move if need be. Sure, he might have been a tad aggressive trying to get answers, and if his mother were here she would've scolded him for his behavior, but he couldn't care less. That was his Olive back there, and he didn't care who he pissed off. He wanted answers.

Lucas must have gotten the picture because he grabbed his coffee and headed over to the receptionist.

Hank couldn't help the small pang of hope that ran through him as he watched his buddy lean against the counter. He knew Lucas was the master sweet talker. If anyone would get him answers it would be him.

His hope was short-lived when he saw the lady shake her head no. When Lucas turned back to him, the pity Hank saw made him snap his head away.

Fuck!

Hank threw himself into his chair as his head started to pound.

How much longer was it going to take for them to hear any news?

Hope was all he had and as every second dwindled by, he lost more and more of it.

Two hours had passed.

Two. More. Fucking. Hours.

During that whole time, not one single person came out to tell him if Olive was alive.

The beep from the surgical ward door sounded once more causing him to jump from his seat. *Let this time be for Olive. Please dear God, let this time be for her*.

When he saw a middle-aged man wearing a surgical outfit

make his way toward the receptionist he jumped from his seat and ran over to the man cutting him off at the pass. "Are you working on Olive Quinn? Do you have any information at all?"

The gentleman moved his attention to Hank, a soulful expression in his eyes. "I'm sorry, sir. But I am not familiar with that patient. I'm sure if you ask at the desk, one of the ladies will be able to get you an update."

Hank spun on his heel as he threw his hands in the air in pure frustration. "You've got to be kidding me." If someone didn't tell him how Olive was in the next five seconds he was going to break down that fucking door and go find her himself.

"We'll do that," Lucas, the voice of reason sounded from next to him.

"I'm tired of talking to her." Hank glared at the receptionist. "She doesn't know shit, and she doesn't want to go back there and find out. It's the same goddamn story every fucking time."

"She's doing her job, Tank. You and I both know there is nothing more she can do."

"It's bullshit and you know it." Hank was done. He stormed over to the desk. "Have you heard anything? Anything at all."

"I'm sorry, sir, but no."

"This is unbelievable." Hank slammed his fist on the counter. "You don't fucking get it. The woman I love is back there and I haven't heard a goddamn thing since she'd been taken back. Fucking *hours*. I'm trying to be patient here, but my patience is running thin." He pointed to the phone. "Call someone and get me some fucking answers."

The receptionist stared at him, before turning her gaze to Lucas. When Lucas gave her a pleading smile, she nodded.

"Let me call back there and see if they finally have any updates."

You've got to be fucking kidding me.

"Thank you, was that so hard?" Hank pushed away from the counter before heading back to his abandoned chair with Lucas following behind him.

"Olive will be okay, man."

"You don't know that. None of us know that." Hank pleaded with his friend as images of the crash flooded his brain. "You saw the car. You were there." Hank looked at his soiled clothes. "There was so much blood."

Lucas' hand clasped around Hank's shoulder as he tried to give him strength. "She's gonna be okay, Hank."

He wanted to believe that. He wanted to believe she'd be okay with every fiber of his being, but at this point, he didn't know if he could. He looked to his friend, begging for him to understand.

When he saw Lucas nod in a small reassurance, Hank leaned back in his chair closing his eyes once again. He'd give anything to go back to that morning.

Of course, he'd never take back telling Olive he loved her, but he would have damn well not walked out on her. What he should have done was thrown her over his shoulder and toss her back onto the bed and make her see without a reasonable doubt, they were meant to be, and that he *did* love her.

No, instead he let his emotions take control and he stormed out of the apartment.

He felt his body cringe. How could he have ended them like that? Especially, when it was said in the heat of the moment, there was no way he meant it.

And right now, as she lay on the surgical table with them doing God knows what to her, the last thing she'd heard from him was how he was done.

He flinched.

Everything was a mess.

When the door beeped again signaling someone was about to come through, Hank didn't bother to look up.

"Olive Quinn?" a middle-aged man in a surgical gown called out.

When the words registered in his head, Hank jumped from his seat and darted over to the doctor. "Right here."

The doctor held out his hand. "I'm Doctor Wyatt. I'm one of the surgeons that worked on Olive."

Hank shook his hand. "Thank you for coming out to update us. I'm Hank Parker, can you tell me how Olive is doing?"

Hank waited impatiently as Doctor Wyatt looked at the file in his hands. "Her chart shows a Miranda and Hank Parker as her emergency contacts." He closed the chart before placing it under his arm. "I'm not going to sugarcoat this for you, Mr. Parker. It shows in the file you're one of our local firefighters, and I'm assuming by the sight of your clothes you know the drill. It was touch and go there for a while. We lost her a few times on the table."

Hank's world vanished around him as the words sunk in. It was like they pierced his soul.

We lost her.

He lost all ability to speak as visions of Olive in a wedding dress played through his mind. He saw her playing with their children in the backyard of a home they'd purchased. The final vision was them sitting in a rocking chair after growing old together as they recounted their memories.

His heart stopped. He could have lost all of that.

"How is she doing?" Lucas asked, taking a step closer to the doctor.

"And, you might be?"

"Olive's soon to be brother in law." He crossed his arms

over his chest. "Can we please cut the crap and you tell us exactly what's going on. Is she okay?"

Doctor Wyatt mimicked his stance. "If and when she wakes up, we'll know more." His expression softened. "In a few hours, we'll reassess. Hopefully, we'll know more then."

If she wakes up? Hank couldn't have heard that right.

"Excuse me?" Lucas' brows shot to the ceiling.

"We'll have to wait and see," Doctor Wyatt continued.

Those words finally snapped Hank to life. "What do you mean we have to wait and see?" Hank felt the blood drain from his face. "You don't know when she'll wake up or *if* she'll wake up?"

The doctor squared his shoulders before taking a deep breath. "I know this is difficult. We are doing everything we can for her at this point. We stopped the intercranial bleed and were able to relieve the pressure on her brain." Doctor Wyatt's expression hardened as he continued the prognosis. "We were also able to stabilize her ribs. However, when her ribs broke from the impact, one of them punctured her left lung."

Hank's heart froze as his eyes scanned the doctor for any sign of possible good news.

"We were able to reinflate the collapsed lung and drain the bleeding from around her heart. Unfortunately, from the impact her abdominal injuries were pretty traumatic causing a ruptured spleen, which we had to remove. Other than heavy bruising, and some additional lacerations on her abdomen, we believe her internal injuries will heal with no further complications. Her worst bruising was from where her seatbelt laid across her body." He stared Hank in the eyes. "That seatbelt saved her life. There is no doubt in my mind she would have gone through the windshield without it."

Saved her life.

Gone through the windshield.

Hank's mind replayed the doctor's words as he tried to make sense of it.

"Ortho was able to set her broken leg." He motioned to Hank's bloodied clothes. "We cleaned up the glass from the lacerations on her head. That along with her busted lip is what caused the majority of the blood loss."

Once the words registered Hank felt his body release a fraction of its tension. The doctor was right. Head wounds always bleed a lot. He knew this. He'd seen it many times throughout his career.

"We have done everything we could do at this point. It's a wait and see game now."

That wasn't good enough for him. He needed to see her with his own eyes, he had to make sure she was still alive. "Where is she? When can I see her?"

"She was just wheeled into recovery. Once we deem she is stable enough we'll get her into a room. I'll have someone come out and get you then."

"How long will that be?" he pleaded with the doctor begging for a more solid answer.

"Your guess is as good as mine, Mr. Parker. Miss Quinn just underwent major surgery. It could be another hour, or ten."

"Ten fucking hours!" Hank stopped himself from punching the man. "That's not good enough. You don't get it."

Lucas grabbed onto Hank's arm pulling him away from the situation. "Thank you, Doc. We appreciate you letting us know how she's doing."

Hank felt like he was about to explode. He did his best to get himself in control as he took Lucas' lead and started moving back to his seat.

What was another few hours?

Olive was alive.

At this point, if it took another twenty years, he'd wait for her. He'd always wait for her.

Before he made it to the chair, Hank turned back to Doctor Wyatt. He took a few steps in his direction, as he pleaded with him. "You're not sure if she's going to wake up, though, right?"

Doctor Wyatt's expression softened. "I'm sorry, but no, with the extent of her head trauma and other injuries, we can't know for certain. However, I can assure you we did everything we could. She's in the best hands now. I'll personally keep an eye on her."

Hank gave him a curt nod. "Thank you."

Hank started walking back to the God-awful chair, he'd claimed for however long it took.

"Hank!"

When Hank turned toward the sound of his name, he saw Miranda running full speed down the corridor toward him.

CHAPTER SEVENTEEN

HANK LOOKED at his watch for what seemed like the hundredth time over the last two days. He didn't know why he kept glancing at it, but he couldn't stop. As each second crept past and Olive laid on the hospital bed, his hope dwindled.

He'd become a shell of himself.

There was no going around it. Every time he looked up and saw Olive's battered body lying there, another part of him died.

Hank slowly moved over to the side of the bed. When he was beside her, he placed his hand on her forehead before he brought his arm around her body gently, making sure not to pull on her IV or breathing tube. He hugged her as cautiously as he could. *I miss you.*

Hank closed his eyes, as he did his best to rein in his raw emotions. He leaned over to kiss her on the cheek. "Hey, baby, it's me again," he whispered into her ear. "I'd really appreciate it if you'd open those gorgeous eyes for me. I miss seeing them spit fire when I've fucked up."

He gently placed his head on hers. "Please, Olive. I need you. Please don't give up."

The knock on the door alerted him to another person in the room.

Hank tensed when he saw it was Miranda. The inquisitive look she gave him had him snap his gaze back to Olive. He didn't know how to act around his sister when it came to Olive. Which was weird to begin with. He wanted to come clean with her, but he knew Olive didn't want that.

"Am I interrupting anything?" Miranda asked, while giving him the once-over. She'd been doing that every time she'd come into the room if he was there. Not waiting for his reply, she moved to the opposite side of Olive's bed.

"No," he answered.

Miranda placed her hand on Olive's giving it a light squeeze.

When Hank saw the tears in his sister's eyes, it was like another punch to the gut. Apart from his mother, the two women he cared most about in his life were hurting and he had no idea how to fix it.

Hank eyed the ceiling sending a plea to anyone that would listen.

Miranda turned her attention from Olive back to him. The pleading expression in her eyes nearly killed him. "Do you think she'll start breathing on her own soon?" Her voice was only above a whisper.

Hank looked down at Olive.

He didn't know.

He prayed she would, but at this point, he didn't have a clue. "We can only hope she will," he answered honestly before he started brushing his hand against the top of Olive's forehead, pushing back some of her unruly hair.

Miranda's head snapped to his as her eyes hardened.

"That's not good enough, Hank. You know about this stuff 'cause of your job. Don't act like you don't. Tell me. Does she have a chance of coming out of this or what?"

How in the hell was he supposed to answer that? Especially when every minute that passed by, he felt Olive slipping away more and more? "I'm not a doctor, Miranda. It can go either way. We have to stay positive, though, she's improved some over the last two days." He willed himself to believe his own words.

Miranda's shoulders slumped in defeat as she moved away from the bed to sit in the vacant seat in the room. The same chair Hank deemed his new home until Olive recovered.

"I should have never left," Miranda broke the silence.

"Don't be silly. You had to leave. Besides, you leaving wouldn't have stopped this from happening." Hank placed his hand on Olive's doing his best to give himself strength.

"You don't know that. If I'd stayed she would have never gotten into her piece of shit car. She would have never gotten into that accident."

The moment he saw Miranda pull into herself with undeserved guilt, his heart tightened. If anyone was guilty in this situation it was him.

It didn't matter the number of times Lucas reminded him the only person at fault was the driver that ran the red light, Hank still wouldn't accept it.

This was his guilt to bear, not Miranda's.

"If Olive were awake she'd throw something at your head and tell you to shove it," he said, as he did his best to lighten the mood.

Thankfully, his attempt made his sister huff out a laugh before a sad smile graced her lips. "She'd probably demand a zombie movie binge watch and tacos."

The visual of that made Hank laugh himself. He was

certain Olive would demand those things. That was his Olive, one second she would be hounding him about something, then the next asking for some horror movie and snacks which mainly focused on tacos.

Hank scrutinized Olive's mangled face, before he bent over and placed a kiss on her forehead. When he looked back up, he saw Miranda staring at him intently. Her head cocked slightly to the side.

"You know, Hank, Olive and I talk every few days, and text non-stop," she started. "When you first moved into the apartment, most of the texts were about how she was planning to murder you in your sleep, and sometimes me for moving out. But, eventually, you stopped coming up…"

Hank stared at her, not exactly sure what to say.

"I hadn't thought much of it," she said. "I mean why would I? Olive's high-strung and overdramatic. I figured things had finally settled down."

"We fell into an easy routine," Hank was quick to interject. He moved his gaze to his sister's. "Plus, as long as I made sure Dog wasn't trying to eat her, things were good."

"Oh yes, I heard all about the vet appointment."

Hank's eyes lit. "Wasn't it awesome?"

Miranda laughed as she nodded her agreement. "From what she told me, I would have to say yes. Only Olive would end up in a situation like that."

"Did she tell you about the Corgi she swears is trying to take over the world?" He smirked at her.

"Pancake?"

Hank barked out a laugh. "Waffles, but close enough."

Once their laughter died out, the room fell silent. Hank once again turned his attention back to Olive.

Squeeze my hand, Olive Oil. Please, he begged as he brushed his thumb against the top of Olive's hand.

"Hank?"

He snapped his attention back to Miranda. The questions danced across her face. He felt his throat tighten as he pulled his gaze from hers and refocused it back to Olive's. "I'm in love with her."

Hank didn't bother looking at his sister. He didn't care what she thought, or who knew he was in love with Olive.

"Since the graduation, right?"

Her words made him stare at her.

"You looked at her differently that day, and every day since," she continued, as she watched his every move.

"I've been in love with her for as long as I can remember," he admitted. "Olive's special. She's the kind of girl you love with your whole heart or nothing at all."

Miranda got up from her seat and made her way over to the opposite side of the hospital bed. "She is special. Olive's one in a million."

"No," Hank corrected. "Olive is one of a kind." He ignored his sister's eyes on him. "She makes me be a better person, Miranda. When I'm with her, I feel like I can do anything. Be anything. She's my other half."

Miranda placed her hand on top of his.

"Do you know how talented she is? Who knew all this time, my little Olive Oil, had an imagination that she could turn into worlds."

"When did you find out about her writing?" she asked.

"I stumbled upon it when I was looking for my keys one day," he answered honestly. "I read all of her books in about three days."

Miranda jerked her head back. "I'm impressed."

"Why? Because I read a book?" He quirked his brow while he chuckled.

"No." Miranda punched his shoulder. "Although, I am a

little surprised you did read. I'm impressed you took the time to read what she's done. And all of them, at that."

"Why wouldn't I?" He turned back to Olive. "When I read her books, I finally got a glimpse of what she'd been hiding away."

The room fell silent, the only sound was the machines keeping Olive alive.

"So, are you two like together?" Miranda asked.

"It's complicated."

"Aren't all relationships?"

Hank's face formed into a lopsided grin.

"More importantly, how could neither of you tell me you were seeing each other?" She crossed her arms over her chest. "I move away and bam I'm left out in the cold?"

"If it were up to me I would have told everyone who I came in contact with. Olive wanted to keep our *shenanigans* a secret."

Miranda rolled her eyes. "Why am I not surprised."

"She puts everything into its proper box. Everything has a place, including her emotions."

"She's been like that since kindergarten," Miranda remarked as she looked at him. "She can't help it."

Miranda focused her gaze back to Olive. "The moment you wake up missy, you and I are having a long heart to heart." She shuddered. "How could you not have told me you were banging my brother? I mean *eww* on all accounts, but what happened to full disclosure between us? Didn't I tell you all about slimeball Jeffrey from the other night?"

"Who's Jeffrey?" Hank growled, before narrowing his eyes at his sister.

"No one for you to be concerned about."

"Miranda..." he warned.

"What dear brother of mine, who is also sleeping with my

best friend and if I didn't think you were perfect for her, I'd knock your bloody lights out?"

"I'm not perfect for her, but I am trying to be." He diverted his attention back to his girl. "We got into a fight right before the car crash. I stormed out of the apartment telling her I didn't want to do this with her anymore."

A sadness filled Miranda's eyes. "What caused the fight?"

"I told her I was in love with her."

"That would have been your first mistake." She held up her finger. "Olive doesn't do *love*. Which doesn't make any sense. The girl can write a love story with the best of them, but when it comes to herself, love isn't real. At least she doesn't think it is."

"It is," he replied. "And I know she loves me too. I just need to help her see that. I should have given her more time to let it sink in. I should have controlled my anger when she threw my love back in my face, but I didn't know how. Instead, the last thing she heard from me was it's over."

"She was probably overwhelmed, Olive needs time to analyze everything. She comes up with elaborate plans in her head as she pieces together her life, step by step."

"I know," he replied. "It's one of the reasons I love her. Her mind is a masterpiece slash war zone that fights zombies, and contemplates the next alien invasion all while dreaming up stories about two people finding each other in this fucked up world."

"That's what makes Olive, Olive." Miranda placed her hand on Olive's shoulder before she turned and made her way back to her seat.

Exactly.

Hank scanned Olive's body as his mind replayed the fight again for the millionth time.

When he went back to the apartment to change that first night, he stood in the living room replaying every second.

He felt pain behind his eyes as he squeezed her hand one more time. "She won't give me her heart, Miranda."

"She will." This time when Miranda looked at him, he saw a hope there he hadn't seen before. "She just has to wake up first."

———

Hank sat beside Olive's bed as he read one of her favorite books out loud to her. Just as he'd done for the last few days. After the first night, he and Miranda started taking shifts so Olive had someone by her side at all times. He was grateful the station offered him as much time as he needed.

He'd pretty much lived in the hospital since Olive was admitted. When he did make it home, he brought back enough clothes so he wouldn't have to worry about leaving her side. With his buddies agreeing to keep an eye on Dog, and Miranda being back in town, he had no reason to.

On the first night Miranda made him go home, he walked into their apartment and instantly noticed Olive's bookshelf. That's when he got the idea to read to her. She pointed out her favorites the day he helped rearrange the bookshelf after the one prank too many drama.

He knew how much getting lost in her worlds meant to her, so he wanted to give her that.

When Hank reached the end of the chapter he looked over at Olive. She was still pretty battered, but some of the smaller bruises had lightened in color.

To him though, the sight of seeing Olive hooked up to the ventilator, and IVs said something else. Doctor Wyatt had sworn she was improving every time he'd come in and evaluated her, but without Hank personally seeing those pretty blue eyes open, he couldn't help his doubt that crept in.

That was the worst part.

He didn't want to live in that doubt. He wanted hope. He wanted to sit back in his chair and know for a fact that Olive would turn to him any moment and call him a jerk for dog-earing her book rather than using the bookmark. Something she considered an ultimate sin.

Hank smirked as he dog-eared the page, before placing the book on the nearby table. He then scooted his chair closer to Olive. "Hey, pretty girl. It's me again. I'm sure you're tired of hearing my voice all the time." He chuckled. "I'm sure it's driving you crazy. Lucas never misses a chance to tell me to shut my trap." With a small sigh, he continued. "Anyway, I wanted to tell you, I love you."

Hank planned on telling her every day. Even if she didn't realize it, he was going to stop at nothing from reminding her of it daily. He took Olive's hand in his giving it a small squeeze. "I miss you, baby, and I need you to wake up. I miss your sassiness, your quirks, your angry huffs that cause the small wrinkles on your forehead." A sad smile formed on his lips. "I miss your little snore you swear you don't make. I miss your smile and all your crazy conspiracy theory ideas. I miss lying next to you and feeling your heartbeat. Most of all baby, I miss you. I need you to wake up for me, Olive Oil. If not for me, then for Miranda. She's been a mess. Or better yet, screw Miranda, wake up for Dog."

Hank brought Olive's hand to his mouth before he lightly kissed it. "Dog really misses you. I don't know if she misses pushing you around or just misses you, but when I went home this morning she refused to get off of your bed." He chuckled. "Get this, she somehow brought her cat bowl up there and demands that's where she'll be fed. I'm still trying to figure out how she managed to get it on the bed, but this is Dog we are talking about." Hank started rubbing his thumb along Olive's hand. "I need you to wake up so Dog can go back to being herself. She's freaking me out."

Hank placed his forehead on the side of the bed, as he did his best to control the rampant emotions that were running through him. "If I could switch places with you, Olive Oil. I would."

Hank pushed himself away from the bed before bringing her hand to his lips once more. After kissing it, he placed it gently on the bed and reached for the book. Hank settled into his seat before starting once more. "Chapter Twelve..."

"Hey, honey."

He looked from the book to see his mother, Robin, walk through the door. A sense of calm washed over him, as it did every time she'd come to visit Olive. "Hey, Mom."

Robin made her way over to the other side of Olive's bed. "How's she doing? Have you heard anything?"

Hank shook his head, before closing the book and placing it back on the table. "The doctor keeps saying she's improving, but I don't know if she really is. To me, improvement means waking up, so I don't know. They said she isn't breathing on her own yet."

"If the doctors say they see signs of improvement then there are," she assured him. "You have to have faith in that, son. Her body has been through a lot. It needs all the rest it can get to heal."

Hank fell back into his chair, before placing his hand over his eyes in desperation. "I know, Mom. I just wish there was more tangible proof she was getting better." He'd take anything at this point.

Robin leaned over the bed placing a small kiss on Olive's cheek. "Hey Olive, it's Momma Parker. You take all the time you need to get better. Don't let Hank pressure you. We'll be right here waiting when you're ready."

Hank shot his eyes to his mother, his lips going into a thin line. "I'm not pressuring her."

Robin stared at her son with both of her brows toward

the roof causing Hank to hold his hands up in surrender. "Okay, I might be mentioning it every ten or so minutes, but I can't help it." He sat back in his chair, defeated.

"I know, sweetie." Robin's voice was soft. "Your heart's in a good place. But no woman wants to be constantly told what to do."

Leave it to his mother to be the voice of reason.

Ignoring the gaze he felt from his mother, he focused his attention back on Olive. It had only been a few days. No one could recover that fast. He needed to keep reminding himself of that.

Robin placed her hand on his. "She's gonna wake up, Hank."

God, he hoped so.

"And when she does, we can talk about wedding plans and grandbabies. I'm not getting any younger, you know?"

That got his attention.

Hank's body stiffened as he turned to his mother. His features must have shown his shock because she shook her head with a tsk. "Do you really think your mother's that dumb?" Robin nonchalantly walked to the chair in the room and sat, before making eye contact with Hank.

He didn't know what to say, so he said nothing.

Robin crossed her left leg over her right before leaning into one side of the chair. "Mother's always know, Hank."

"How?"

Robin cocked her brow at him. "You've never been good at hiding your feelings, honey. Your father and I've known you've had a thing for Olive Quinn since you were kids."

Hank's mouth nearly hit the floor.

"Wipe that look off your face young man."

At his mother's playful tone, he chuckled. "I can't. This is just how my face is."

"Truly a face only a mother could love, no doubt," Robin joked.

"Hey!"

With a quick shrug, Robin ignored Hank's appalled face and looked back to Olive. "I'm glad you have her, Hank. I've always loved her as if she were my own."

"I know you have, Mom."

"It's nice to see two people so in love," she said.

"She doesn't think I'm really in love with her, Mom," he spoke truthfully. "But, I can guarantee you as soon as she wakes up I'll stop at nothing to prove to her how much I do love her. She'll eventually see she loves me too."

"I have no doubt, Hank." Robin pulled out a wedding magazine from her bag and started thumbing through it. "You've always been one not to stop once you've set your sights on something."

After seeing what his mother was looking at, Hank couldn't help but roll his eyes. Either she'd talked to Miranda, or she planned this all along.

Knowing his family, he was sure it was a combination of both.

He shrugged it off as he turned his focus back on Olive. His mother was right about one thing, once he had his sights set, nothing was going to stop him.

Olive's "love doesn't exist" be damned.

Hank was going to prove to her and anyone else that doubted him what love was really about. As soon as she opened her eyes, he was going to show her the adventure of a lifetime. Dog included.

He sat back in his chair with a smile on his face. It was funny how speaking with his mom for only a few minutes could change his whole outlook.

He *knew* Olive was going to wake up and when she did it was game time.

He reached for the book ready to continue reading her the story.

That's when Mr. and Mrs. Quinn walked in.

CHAPTER EIGHTEEN

WHAT THE HELL is that annoying beeping?

Olive felt a pounding in her head, but her hand wouldn't move to reach for it. *What in the hell is going on?*

The beeping started to get louder which in turn made her head throb.

Holy crap that's annoying!

Olive tried to lift her hand again, but had no such luck. *I hope someone got the license plate of the truck that ran over me, because they decided they forgot something and backed over me again. Then for good measure, ran over me one more time.*

Olive tried to piece together what was going on. Her throat was dry and scratchy, and no matter how hard she tried to move she wasn't going anywhere. She decided to give up moving her limbs, and focused on her eyes. When she realized she was still surrounded by darkness, she panicked.

Why can't I open my eyes?

She heard the beep again which snapped her brain into gear. *Oh, dear God. This is it. This is the alien mothership and I've finally been abducted.* Olive started overreacting. *I bet I'm one of their experiments. If I could just open my eyes I could finally catch a glimpse of what they look like...*

"I see you finally decided to show up?"

What do you mean 'decided to show up?' You all are the ones that abducted me. I wonder if they can hear my thoughts? Hello! I come in peace. Unless peace on your planet means something different than it does where I'm from. Then I come in whatever you consider not be hostile.

Olive tried to open her eyes once more but they refused to budge. *Give me a break!*

"I called you when she was rushed into surgery. If you weren't going to show up then, why even bother now? *Days later.*"

Alien man sounds pissed.

As Olive tried to make her brain function, she realized there was something familiar about the voice. The sound weirdly comforted her, but she couldn't figure out why. *Strange.*

"She's our daughter, of course, we are going to show up," another familiar voice said. However, this one didn't give her a comforting feeling. No, this one made her want to hide.

"Mrs. Quinn, I hate to interject here, but as a mother, if someone called and informed me my child had been in an accident nothing would have stopped me from getting to them."

"It's nice to see you again, Robin," the voice spoke with a hint of disgust. "For your information, when we received the news we were in the middle of an event. You couldn't expect us to leave, now could you?"

"Yes, we could have. She's you're fuckin' daughter," this came from alien man.

What in the world is going on?

"From what you described, it didn't sound like she would have made it out of surgery."

Surgery?

"Sorry to disappoint you, but she did," alien man snarled. "It's nice of you to finally make your presence known."

Presents? Who's getting gifts? Olive's head had never hurt this bad in her life.

She heard rustling around her until a new voice spoke up, a deeper voice. "How long do they plan on keeping her on there? I guess it's not uncommon for people to live off of a ventilator, although if you ask me it's a waste of resources."

"How could you say such a thing, Mr. Quinn?"

"Do you expect anything less from them, Mom? When it comes to Olive, they have never been parents. They're nothing but a sad sack of humans if you ask me."

Hank? Why does that sound so much like Hank?

She tried once again to open her eyes, but it was like there was a disconnect between her brain and body.

"Do not speak to me like that."

"Like what? The piece of garbage you both are?"

"Let's take a deep breath. Everyone needs to calm down."

Mamma Parker?

"Calm down my ass! Their daughter is fighting for her life right there and they can't seem to be bothered."

Fighting for my life...

Just like that, everything came rushing back to Olive. She remembered spending the morning in bed with Hank, they had talked about a lot of things. Her parents and her obsession with the holidays. Then there was Hank declaring he was in love with her.

The fight!

Hank had told her he didn't want to be with her anymore.

Olive started to feel her body and mind connect, but it wasn't quite there.

I'm in love with Hank Parker!

Images of Olive realizing she was in love with Hank

started to flood through her mind. She recalled declaring her love for him and having to tell him right away. She took the chance and got into her car...

The accident.

No, Olive wasn't on an alien spacecraft. She was in the hospital.

Hank was there.

Her Hank.

Olive thought she'd finally gained enough sense to control her body. A wash of terror ran through her when she tried to speak but she couldn't.

She started frantically moving her fingers begging for anyone to notice.

Please, Hank, look at me. I'm stuck, but I'm here.

Olive's body rushed into a panic.

"What's going on?" Olive recognized Robin's voice.

She felt someone grab onto the hand she'd been moving. It was an instant calm that washed over her. "That's it, baby, stay calm for me," Hank spoke gently.

Hank!

"She's waking up," Hank hollered. "Call the doctor!"

Olive felt Hank kiss her forehead. "You're okay, Olive Oil. Someone's coming."

At the sound of his voice, the panic she'd felt about not being able to speak started to subside.

"I know it's hard, but can you try and open your pretty blue eyes for me, baby?"

She thought she had been trying. Wasn't she?

"Please, Olive, I need to see your eyes again."

The plea in his voice had Olive mustering all her strength. She could do this. As long as Hank was there, she could do anything. Even though her eyelids felt like lead weights were attached, she pushed as hard as she could. Olive managed to flutter them open briefly before closing them right away.

Too bright!

"That's it, Olive. Open those eyes for me." Olive heard Hank's voice change direction and addressed someone else. "Turn the lights down."

Why can't I breathe? Olive bit down against the tube in her mouth.

"Don't struggle. As soon as the doctor comes in we'll get the tube out. Try to stay calm, sweet girl."

Stay calm? As soon as she was able to gain full strength of her body she was going to punch him. You don't tell someone to stay calm when they have a tube down their throat, and they are struggling to open their eyes.

Stay calm my ass...

Olive tried to blink a few times before she was finally able to fully open her eyes. Once the haze started to fade, Hank's face finally came into view.

Hank had tears in his eyes as he looked down at her. His skin was a bit blotchy and he could use a good shave. He looked like he'd been through hell, but nonetheless, he looked perfect to her.

I love you, she tried saying, but the tube hindered her. She felt her panic start to rise as she tried fighting through the plastic.

"Shh, baby, as soon as the doctor is here, we'll take out the tube." Hank made her focus all her attention on him.

"It seems to me we came at just the right moment." Olive snapped her eyes to the voice. When her mother came into view, she almost recoiled.

"Better late than never," her father chimed in.

Better late than never? Are you kidding me? I'm their child.

"Get out!" Hank snapped. "Get the fuck out."

"We're not going anywhere, she's our daughter."

"You didn't seem to care about that fact when she died on the way here or the multiple times she died on the operating table. Now, get the fuck out, before I take you out myself."

"Hank, calm down, no matter how angry you are at how they reacted to the situation, they are still Olive's parents. Let's wait until the doctor comes in. We don't need to stress Olive out any more than she already is," Robin said, defusing the situation.

"It's nice to finally see those eyes, young lady." A doctor Olive had never seen before stormed into the room. "I'm Dr. Wyatt, it's nice to see you back in the land of the living. You had us worried there for a little while."

Olive watched Doctor Wyatt move to the opposite bedside of Hank. "I don't think I saw this man leave your side." The doctor nodded his head toward Hank.

Olive moved her gaze from the doctor, who was now poking and prodding her, to Hank. *He hadn't left my side?*

"I'm sure you want to get that breathing tube out, now don't cha?" the doctor asked, causing her to focus her attention back on him. "I'm going to ask everyone to leave the room, while we get this tube out and then do a quick evaluation."

"I'm not leaving her," Hank stated. There was absolutely no question in his voice.

Olive watched as Doctor Wyatt regarded Hank for a few moments, before giving a quick nod. "I'll only allow it because every time you move your hand away from hers, her heart rate increases."

To test his theory the doctor reached over the bed, and pushed Hank's hand off of Olive's. Instantly, her heart rate increased. Hank grabbed onto her hand, before shooting daggers at the doctor. "Do it again and I'll murder you."

Forever a charmer.

Olive rolled her eyes. However, she wanted to get this

show on the road. She could only control her panic for so long with a tube down her throat.

Doctor Wyatt held his hands in surrender. "No need for hostility, Mr. Parker. I noticed it when I did my rounds yesterday and this morning. When you're holding her, she seems calmer. Why do you think I kept telling you she was improving?"

Umm hello! I'm still here. Can you have this conversation after *you've taken this giant ass tube out of my throat?*

Hank growled.

Oh, for the love of all things!

The doctor winked at Hank purposely riling him up. "I would have let you stay in the room regardless. Your medical training is sufficient enough."

I think this doctor has a death wish.

"If *he* can stay in the room, *I'm* staying in the room. I'm her mother," Mrs. Quinn voiced her opinion.

Olive wanted to pump her fist in the air when she watched Doctor Wyatt cock his head slightly to the side. "Oh, my apologies. I mistakenly thought this lovely woman was her mother." He pointed toward Robin. "I haven't seen you here at all."

"My husband and I were detained."

Doctor Wyatt's brows rose before he shrugged. "Doesn't matter. Out you go." He opened his arms and nearly shoved everyone out of the room.

As Robin left, she addressed Hank. "I'm going to call Miranda and tell her Olive's awake."

After another small protest from Olive's mother about leaving, and a grumble about how they should have waited another hour, the doctor was able to clear the room except for Hank and the nurses.

"You ready, Olive?"

Olive did her best to nod.

"I'm going to have Mr. Parker step back for a few seconds while I take the tube out." Doctor Wyatt reached for a new pair of gloves before donning them. "Have you ever gotten the wind knocked out of you?" he asked.

Olive's eyes widened. *Once. And it sucked more than anything,* she thought.

"She fell out of the treehouse in our backyard when we were younger," Hank answered for her.

Olive looked at the doctor, and then back at Hank. *What he said.*

"It's going to be close to that. You'll cough but don't be alarmed, it's completely normal." Before she knew it, Olive had the doctor right over her and the nurse next to him. A gush of wind filled her lungs as the tube was removed causing her to cough uncontrollably.

Holy shit on a cracker that hurt.

As Olive tried to regain her bearings she felt someone grab her hand. When she looked, Hank gave her a sweet smile.

She opened her mouth, but he silenced her with a swift kiss. "Don't speak. Your throat's bound to be dry and scratchy. Let me get you some ice chips." He turned to the bedside table next to him and picked up his water.

"No hanky panky," Doctor Wyatt joked. "Let the poor girl breathe on her own before you try to resuscitate her again."

Olive smiled. She liked this doctor. She liked him a hell of a lot more because he got under Hank's skin.

"I'm sure you've got many questions," Doctor Wyatt remarked. "But before we go any further, tell me what do you remember?"

CHAPTER NINETEEN

HANK HAD NEVER BEEN MORE thankful for his mother, then he was right now. After the doctor evaluated Olive and given the all clear for everyone to come back in the room, his mother had somehow convinced Mr. and Mrs. Quinn to grab a bite to eat instead. Thank God, because right now he needed some time with his girl.

From the moment the doctor left the room, Olive hadn't taken her eyes off of him.

Add that to the list of things he was thankful for.

When he looked into Olive's eyes, he saw the questions she had there, but more importantly, he saw her longing.

As Hank stood over her, he let his eyes roam over her still broken and bruised body. As his eyes drank her in, he swore she never looked more beautiful than she did right now.

Olive was awake.

His heart did a strange flipflop, as his face broke into a smile.

"Wh-when," she started to say in a rasped voice. "When you stare at me like that it makes me feel weird."

Hearing her voice was like music to his ears. "Is there another way you want me to stare at you?" he asked.

Olive narrowed her eyes at him before she gave up and threw her head back onto her pillow forcefully.

When Hank saw her face scrunch in discomfort he placed his hand under her chin forcing her to look his way. "The doctor said he'd get the nurse to bring you some pain meds."

She faced him before giving him a small nod.

Seeing Olive in pain was killing him.

He wanted to be able to give her some sort of comfort so he leaned over her, before resting his head on her forehead.

Olive was alive. He thanked God for the millionth time.

He placed a swift kiss on her lips, being cautious of her cut. "Thank you," he whispered. "Thank you for not giving up."

When Olive tried to speak he silenced her with another kiss. "Shh. I know we have a lot to talk about, and we will, but right now I want to enjoy this moment." He kissed her again.

However, the second he felt Olive bite his bottom lip he jerked back. "What the hell was that for?"

"Trying to keep me quiet by kissing me." She glared at him. "I do not appreciate being manipulated."

Was it wrong he thought her rasped voice was sexy? Probably. He shook his head. Leave it to Olive to be as feisty as ever even after everything she'd been through. "I'm not manipulating you," he protested.

"Yes, you are." Olive tried to push herself further up on the bed, but ultimately failed.

"Why are you so goddam stubborn?" Hank rolled his eyes before grabbing onto her waist hoisting her to her desired position in seconds. When he saw her wince again he cringed.

Shit.

"I'm not the stubborn one, *you* are." Olive narrowed her eyes at him. "And, that's one of the many reasons I love you."

Hank froze.

Did he hear her correct?

She loved him.

Olive placed her hands on her lap and stared at them as she began to fidget. "I'm so sorry, Hank. I am sorry for everything."

He watched her in complete awe as tears ran down her cheeks.

She loves me?

"You will never know how truly sorry I am, Hank. After you told me you loved me I freaked. Within seconds everything I thought I knew flipped upside down and I couldn't handle it." Olive focused her gaze from her hands to him. "I didn't know what it felt like to be loved, at least I thought I didn't."

"I've loved you for a long time," he finally said.

"I know that now. I know that even though I never thought I deserved love, I'm lucky enough to have found it." Her chin trembled. "I was on my way to tell you. I had to tell you. I couldn't go on another second with you thinking I wasn't in love with you too." Her body slumped into itself. "Then when you said you were done... I-I-"

"I should have never said that." Hank gently wiped away the tears from her cheeks. "I can never be done with you, Olive. You're my whole world."

"I thought I lost you." The look she gave him broke him in two. "I knew my car wasn't the safest, but the idea of you walking away and never coming back killed me. I had to get to you."

"Shh," he tried his best to calm her. "It's okay, baby. You're okay. That's all that matters."

He wanted to keep her calm, however, Olive seemed to

have different plans.

She clearly needed to tell her side of the story and no matter how bad it might hurt, he had to sit there and listen to it.

"The car came out of nowhere," she whispered as a new wave of tears started. "Right before everything went black, I saw your face. I would have given everything at that moment to make sure you knew I loved you. I reached out for you, but then you were gone."

God damn. Hank's insides were ripped apart as Olive recanted her memories from the accident. The fear she must have felt, the pain, the unknowing. He vowed at that moment he would do everything within his power to make sure she never felt that way again.

Being careful not to hurt her, Hank cupped her face in his hands. "I'm so sorry, baby. I'm so fucking sorry you had to go through any of that. And, I'm even more sorry you're lying here in pain right now. I should have never left the way I did. Not when I knew I didn't mean those words. Olive, I have been in love with you for a very long time. Even if you had tried to kick me out of the apartment I would have still fought for you. I'm just sorry my dumb ass forced you to get into that death trap of a car. But in all of this, there is one thing I am grateful for."

"What?" she whispered.

"I'm grateful that I can stand here next to you and tell you, I love you."

Olive's face brightened. "I love you, too."

Hank leaned over and kissed her, pouring all of his emotions into their embrace.

"Didn't I tell you to let the poor girl breathe?" Doctor Wyatt interrupted them as he came into the room, a nurse right next to him. "I leave the room for ten minutes and you're already trying to block her airways."

Hank growled at Doctor Wyatt before he turned away with a shrug. "I was telling my girl I love her."

"Tell her vocally for a while until she's got her breathing under control. The poor girl's been on a ventilator for days. Slow your roll." Doctor Wyatt winked at Hank.

Bastard!

Hank's lips thinned as he watched the doctor work. He knew Doctor Wyatt was right, but could you blame him? Not only was Olive awake, but she'd also told him she was in love with him.

He'd be damned if he wasn't going to kiss her.

"Hank doesn't follow the rules much," Olive remarked, as she sent a teasing smile his way.

The fact that her busted lip made her smile a little lopsided had him smirking. He couldn't be mad at her. Not when seeing her eyes shine with love at him was the best sight he'd ever seen.

"I've prescribed some extra pain medicine to help you." He looked at her chart at the end of her bed. "Once these kick in, you'll more than likely fall asleep. Sleep is good. It'll help your body heal."

Olive nodded as the nurse injected some medicine into her IV.

"I'll be back in a few hours to check on you," Doctor Wyatt announced before placing her chart back at the end of her bed. "Try and limit the tonsil hockey for a little while."

"I'll do my best to control him, but like I said, he doesn't follow the rules well," Olive joked as Doctor Wyatt and the nurse left the room.

"I like him. He's fun," she said when she looked at Hank.

"He's a pain in the ass if you ask me," Hank grumbled. "He's got too many jokes. But he saved your life, so I'll let it slide."

"How noble of you."

Hank puffed out his chest. "Damn right."

Olive started fidgeting with her sheet, causing Hank's brows to knit. "What is it, baby?"

Olive's faced pained for a second before she took a deep breath. "How's the other driver? Are they okay?"

Her words were like a punch to the gut. He knew it was coming, it was in Olive's nature to make sure everyone was always accounted for and okay, but he'd wished he didn't have to tell her so soon. He took a deep breath before he grabbed onto her hand. "I'm sorry baby, but the other driver didn't make it."

Olive gasped, which made his heart constrict harder. "No," she said as new tears formed in her eyes.

"When we pulled up to the accident-"

"Hank, no," she stopped him. "Please tell me it wasn't your station. Please, I won't ever be able to live with myself."

Seeing her distress, Hank sat on the side of the bed before pulling her into his arms. "You have no idea how grateful I am it was us that got the call. Rick and Tim are the best goddamn medics this city has. The moment we realized it was you they stopped at nothing to save you."

"I'm so sorry."

"Don't, Olive." He pushed away a stray piece of hair from her face. "Do not be sorry. None of this was your fault. Not even a second of it. That driver ran a red light. Even if your car were in top shape no one would have been able to stop in time."

Her doe eyes staring at him, did him in. "The other driver was gone before we got there, Olive."

Her whole body tensed. "There was nothing anyone could have done, baby. I'm sorry."

Olive nodded, but he knew she didn't accept it. He'd seen this before throughout his career. Even though she wasn't at fault, he knew the guilt would eat at her. As he watched her face contort in pain he vowed he would do whatever it took to make her see she wasn't at fault for this.

"It's good to see you awake, Olive."

Hank snapped his head to the door only to see Olive's parents walk in with his mother.

Robin had a sad smile on her face with her eyes relaying a plea of 'I tried'.

Hank took a deep breath readying himself for whatever hell storm was about to come. He turned his body away from Olive, before taking a few steps up the bed, almost putting her behind him, so he could protect her.

"Mother." Olive skeptically looked at both of her parents. "Thank you for coming."

Hank hated how proper Olive forced herself to sound.

His hand clenched at his side. The fact she couldn't be herself around her own parents had him wanting to punch the nearest wall.

"Yes," her mother answered. "We had to rearrange some things, but we came as soon as we could."

"Days later," Hank growled.

"And why are you here?" Her mother turned to Hank. "There is no reason for you to be wasting your time here with her."

"Wasting my time?" Hank snapped. *Were these people fucking crazy?*

"I'm sure you've got more important things to do than to keep *her* company." She pointed at Olive.

"I can assure you, Mrs. Quinn, Olive is the most important *thing* to me. Nothing could have kept me away. Too bad, I can't say the same for you."

"What is that supposed to mean?"

"Exactly what I said."

"Please," Olive pleaded with the room. "Can we not do this right now. I'm begging you."

Hank pivoted to see Olive staring at him, a pained expression on her face.

Fuck. How the hell was he supposed to make Olive feel better, but not chew her parents out for being garbage human beings?

"Yes, why don't you run along. *We're* her parents, we can take it from here." Mrs. Quinn moved to the other side of Olive's bed. "We have a lot to talk about."

Olive snapped her head toward her mother. Her left brow cocked. "We do?"

"Of course, Olive," she said. "We only have a few days to file the first claims against your accident. There could be big money here." She had a smug expression on her face. "While the doctor was evaluating you, I called our lawyer."

"You have got to be fucking kidding me!" The words were taken right out of Hank's mouth as he snapped his head to the door.

Miranda stormed into the room, throwing her bag into the nearby chair. "You are some fucking piece of work, Mrs. Quinn."

"Do not talk to me like that," Olive's mother sneered toward Miranda.

That only caused Miranda to cross her arms over her chest before she quirked her left brow. "Like what? The god-awful parent you are?"

"Miranda..." Olive managed to speak.

Hank's sister turned toward her best friend with tears in her eyes. "Once you get better I am going to kick your ass. You have no idea how worried I've been."

At the sight of Miranda, Olive's tears were back.

"No, you don't get to cry." Miranda pointed at her chest. "*I* get to cry, and then I get to beat your ass for taking your car in the first place."

"I'm sorry," Olive sobbed. She extended her arms in the

air begging for Miranda to walk into them.

Miranda saw zero problems with that because she pushed Olive's mother out of the way without a care in the world as she gladly walked into her best friend's arms.

"Didn't I just say you don't get to cry?"

"Shut up!"

Hank watched as Olive did her best to pull Miranda into her arms.

"Excuse me," Mr. Quinn bellowed into the room. "Are you going to let her talk like that to my wife?"

"Your wife?" Hank asked, as his blood boiled. "Even after all the shit your *daughter* has been through the past few days, you're more concerned about *your wife?*"

"No one is going to talk to her like that."

"That's right," Hank stated. "I'm going to talk to her a lot worse than that."

He turned toward Olive's mother. "Get the fuck out."

"I beg your pardon?" Mrs. Quinn placed her hand over her chest.

"You heard me, get the fuck out. No one wants you here, and more importantly, *you* don't want to be here. You never did."

Mrs. Quinn turned toward her daughter. "Olive you are not going to let these hoodlums speak to us like this are you?"

"Hoodlums?" Robin chimed in. "My children are so far from hoodlums it's not even funny."

Hank watched as Olive gently pushed Miranda out of her arms to get an unobstructed view of her mother.

"Did you just call my best friend and boyfriend hoodlums?"

At the word boyfriend, Mrs. Quinn paled. "Your *boyfriend?* Don't be silly, Olive. I know you hit your head pretty hard, but there is no way Hank Parker is your boyfriend."

Hank had never wanted to hit a lady more than he wanted

to hit Olive's mother right now.

"What do you mean he couldn't be my boyfriend?" Olive asked, as shock resonated off her face.

"Exactly that dear, no man like him would even remotely be interested in someone like you. Now, all you need to do is send these little people away and we can get to work on what's important."

Olive's face scrunched as her eyes narrowed on her mother's. "And what's important?"

"Why are you so dense? I already told you. Our lawyer will be here within the hour."

Olive's fists clenched as her breathing increased. "Get out," she growled. "Get the hell out of this room."

"Olive Quinn, I am your mother. Do not talk to me like that."

"You're wrong," Olive snapped. "You've never been a mother to me. The only motherly figure I've had in my life is standing in the corner." She pointed to Robin. "I've never been good enough for you or dad. Never. I used to feel bad about it, I used to do whatever I could to make you both proud of me, but it would always end up the same. I'm your total disappointment. Well, guess what? Not anymore. You're *my* disappointment. I've lived my life in fear of your judgment for far too long."

Olive grabbed onto Hank's hand and pulled him to her. "I don't know how or why, but I'm in love with Hank and I'm lucky enough he loves me too. Lord knows, I never had a good example of what love really is. And, for you to once again throw your judgment on me concerning Hank proves to me you've never loved me. Your judgment doesn't rule me anymore."

Hank squeezed Olive's hand. He'd never been prouder of her than he was at that moment.

"I don't want your lawyer here," Olive continued. "And

more importantly, I don't want either of you here. Now get out."

Mrs. Quinn glared at her daughter. "You ungrateful bitch."

"Don't even think about it," Hank interrupted. "If I were you I'd leave while I still had the chance."

"Is that a threat young man?" Mr. Quinn asked.

"It's a promise."

"I knew we should have never come," Olive's mother said to her husband. "She's always been a waste. The one time she could actually see some profit from this opportunity she will no doubt mess that up too. Let's go dear, there is no point in trying to reason with incompetence." Mrs. Quinn grabbed her bag and flung it over her shoulder.

When they made it to the door Olive called out, "Oh, and one more thing..." The moment her parents turned toward her Olive smiled as wide as she could. "I write romance books with sex scenes that could make a nun blush. Have fun with the rest of your life knowing your daughter writes pantie dropping, pussy weeping, fuck me harder, I'm gonna come all over your face, books."

The room erupted in laughter, Hank didn't even try to hold back his laugh as Mrs. Quinn's mouth dropped open. He would never forget that image for the rest of his life.

With one last huff, Olive's mother stormed out of the hospital room, with Mr. Quinn right on her tail.

"Well, okay then." Robin coughed.

Olive's eyes widened as she looked at his mother. Even through her bruised face he could see the blush creep up her cheeks. "Umm..."

"They're great, Mom," Miranda jumped in. "I mean I will never ever in a million years let you read them because eww, but they are fantastic."

"That's nice, sweetie." Robin nodded at her daughter, before turning to Olive. "We'll talk once you're better."

"Uhh, sure." Olive shied away from Robin as she did her best to hide her embarrassment.

"Come on, Miranda, time to go." Robin pulled on her daughter's arms.

"I'm not leaving I just got here," Miranda protested.

"Yes, you are, young lady. You and I are going to the cafeteria to grab a coffee. Give your brother and Olive a few minutes. A lot just happened."

Miranda glared at Hank. "You do not get to steal my best friend from me. I'm warning you."

Hank held up his hands in surrender. "I'm not."

"You are, but I swear to God if you do anything to hurt her ever, I will murder you in your sleep."

"Miranda," Olive warned which caused Miranda to turn her body to her. "And that's another thing, missy. As soon, and I mean as soon as you're better I'm kicking your ass from here to Timbuktu. Why in the hell did you not tell me you were *sleeping* with my brother? My freakin' brother of all people."

Olive's eye's shot open in surprise. "Your mother is right there!"

"Don't worry honey, Hank told me all about your relationship when you were still unconscious."

Olive threw her head in her hands. "Universe, if you have any sort of mercy in you, will you send down your favorite alien race and have them take me away. I don't care which one, any would do."

Hank burst out laughing as his mother wrangled his sister out of the room, with some additional choice words from her threatening to be back in exactly one hour.

When it was just him and Olive, Hank grabbed onto her waist before he carefully pushed her to one side of the bed.

"What are you doing?" Olive asked, trying to adjust herself the best she could.

"Shh." He toed off his shoes before crawling into the bed with her. There wasn't much room, and he knew Olive needed to be comfortable, but he had to be near her.

"I'm so proud of you," he whispered once he adjusted himself so he wasn't hurting her in any way.

After a few minutes of protest, Olive settled into the bed, curling her battered body around his. "Why?"

"Because today you didn't need the sight of a Christmas tree to remind you to be who you are." He kissed her cheek. "Plus, you told me you love me."

Olive threw her head back onto the pillow with a wince. "And your mom heard about us, *and* found out I write sexy books."

Hank shrugged. "Who cares."

Hank laid his head in the crook of Olive's neck as he molded his body to hers. This was what heaven felt like. And he was going to spend the rest of his life doing whatever he could to make sure Olive knew she was always loved. Hank pulled his head away briefly to kiss her cheek. "I love you, Olive."

"I love you too, Hank. You're a pain in my ass, but I love you too."

"Good." He placed his head back into the crook of her neck. "Remember that when you're healed and I've got you bent over my knee."

He felt Olive push away from him. "What?"

Hank ignored her outrage as a smile spread across his face. He didn't have to look at Olive to know she was glaring at him. "We have the matter of you driving your car which you knew wasn't safe to deal with."

When he heard Olive mumble some choice words in his direction, he sunk deeper into her side a smirk gracing his face.

His work here was done.

CHAPTER TWENTY

OLIVE'S LIFE had somewhat settled down after waking in the hospital two weeks ago. Well, it was as settled as it could be. Olive couldn't really settle when her hospital room was the equivalent to *Grand Central Station*.

She was looking forward to being discharged today. Maybe now she'd get some much needed alone time.

The past two weeks had been far too "people-y" for her.

She did have to admit though; her excess human interaction wasn't too bad. It was nice that Miranda had taken a leave of absence from work to be with her. Most nights ended up being a slumber party just like they had when they were kids.

Although, there was the addition of Hank the nights he wasn't working. Those nights also seemed to come with Rick, Tim, and Lucas.

At this point, Olive joked about making a sign to put on the door saying, "open for business." *She* thought it was funny. Hank not so much.

Then there were also Hank's parents always stopping in.

It was refreshing in a way. She'd never had the "parent" nurturing aspect before.

She liked it.

Between Robin and her need to mother everything and everyone, and Hank's father Jim going out of his way to make the worst dad jokes he could muster in order to make Olive smile, she found herself being loved.

A kind of love she never really felt before, well at least that she'd never realized existed.

As for her own parents, Olive hadn't heard anything from them. She wasn't all that surprised.

The look on her mother's face after she found out what Olive did for a living was priceless. Olive would be shocked if she ever heard from them again. She went against everything they believed in.

Although, there was a small part of Olive that hurt because her parents so readily threw her away, there was another side of her that finally felt free.

Free to be herself.

Plus, with the amount of love coming from the people surrounding her, what more could someone ask for?

Who needed their biological parents when she had people who really loved her?

"We're here to spring ya," Lucas announced as him, Hank, and Miranda walked into Olive's room.

Olive sat on the edge of the bed with a smile on her face. The nurse had unhooked her from the machines thirty minutes ago, before helping her get dressed.

She turned her eyes to Hank. "I'm a little in shock you didn't bring the whole calvary."

"Tim's getting the car, while the rest are at the apartment." Hank's face lit with one of the cockiest smiles she'd ever seen.

"Oh jeez." Olive rolled her eyes. "You do know that's not necessary right?"

Miranda sat on the bed beside her. "We are talking about the same person here aren't we?" She pointed at her brother.

"Yeah," Lucas chimed in. "We're here to make sure he doesn't forget something important."

Olive's face beamed. "And what could that be?"

"Knowing his track record, I wouldn't put it past him to forget *you*. We would have been here twenty minutes ago if he hadn't lost his keys." Lucas smirked in her direction.

"Screw you." Hank punched his friend on the shoulder. "You know damn well I'd never forget her."

"I believe you." He held up his hands in surrender. "I have twenty bucks saying you don't. That's why I'm here."

"To protect your investment?" Miranda laughed which caused Lucas to shoot a wink her way. "Don't I know it."

Olive sat back on the bed and observed the chaos around her as Lucas and Miranda started going in on Hank. Sure, she was still in a fair amount of pain, and although most of her bruises were healing nicely she still had a decent road to recovery left.

She'd come pretty far the last two weeks. And, with the doctor's encouragement and reassurance, she knew she was ready to leave. Even if her broken leg made it difficult to do anything, let alone walk on her own.

She was still too weak for crutches, but they were going to send her home with them. Apparently, having a live-in boyfriend that was also medically trained made Doctor Wyatt give Hank the all clear to be in charge of her recovery plan.

Lord help her.

"You ready to go home?" Hank pulled her attention away from her battered body.

"I am." She gave him a small smile. "Thanks for picking me up."

"I wouldn't have forgotten you." He placed his hand over his chest like he'd been shot. "Do you not have any faith in your man?"

Olive shrugged. "If you were another twenty minutes late I would have won the bet."

"Oh, you are gonna get it," he growled before he brought his lips down to hers in a hungry kiss. "I'm keeping a running tab. I think you're up to fifty-six now."

Olive pulled back in shock. "The heck you say?"

"What a sad day it is to see my favorite patient and her rambunctious posse leave." Doctor Wyatt strolled into the room.

"Didn't you threaten to send me to the psych ward the other night?" Lucas asked.

The doctor smiled at him with his brow cocked. "It wasn't a threat."

"That hurts, Doc. I thought we'd become best friends over the last two weeks."

"Why yes, you and your friends rearranging all the supplies in the stock room was loads of fun. Remind me to put you at the top of my Christmas card list, since we're best friends now."

"I'll be glad to." Lucas stood straighter with a new sense of pride written all over him.

Doctor Wyatt shook his head before he turned his attention to Olive. "Are you sure you want to go home? It'll probably be safer here and less chaotic."

Olive grabbed onto Hank's hand before giving it a squeeze. "I'm positive."

With a reluctant sigh, Doctor Wyatt continued. "Fine, have it your way." He started scribbling notes on his clipboard. "I know we've talked about it already and you're all set to be discharged. Do you have any other questions for me?"

"Nope."

"Okay then, I release you to the care of one Hank Parker." He pointed at Hank. "Listen to him. He's got your recovery plan already memorized. He'll have you walking on your crutches in no time."

Olive groaned. "Can you pretend he isn't qualified. I don't want to listen to him bossing me around. Can't I just go to rehab like everyone else?"

"You're still going to rehab," Doctor Wyatt announced. "He's just gonna make sure you follow through. I now relinquish my power to him." He handed some papers to Hank.

"Is it too much to ask for you to start the zombie apocalypse before we leave? I'm sure you have the altered DNA strand somewhere in the hospital. No one will question it if you accidentally grab the wrong syringe."

"And, that right there is why you are my favorite patient."

Olive sighed. "Not so favorite that you'd do it?"

"If I had the magic string like you say, I'd do it for you."

"That's all I can ask."

"Hey." Hank pulled Olive closer to him. "Stop trying to poach my woman. Get your own nutjob. She's mine."

"Did you just call me a nutjob?"

"Conspiracy theorist, nutjob, they are one in the same," Lucas remarked, coming in to defend Hank.

"Neither one of you call her a nut job," Miranda growled. "Olive might have her quirks, but I will throat punch either one of you in a heartbeat if you try and rile her up."

"Did anyone ever tell you, you're sexy when you defend your delusional friend?" Lucas looked Miranda up and down.

"Excuse me while I vomit." Miranda threw her hand over her mouth.

"And with that, it's time for me to say so long." Doctor Wyatt placed the clipboard under his arm. "You've got your follow up appointments already scheduled. Take it easy and listen to him." He pointed at Hank. "He's in charge."

"Damn right I'm in charge." Hank puffed out his chest.

"Any moment now," Olive yelled out to the doctor as he left the room laughing. She then turned back to Hank. With all the strength she could muster she punched him in the arm.

Ouch, that hurt. When she saw Hank's face morph into surprise she smiled. *Worth it.*

"What the hell was that for?" he asked, faking hurt.

"You called me a nutjob. You're not the only one keeping a running tab."

"I only said that to scare him off. He was getting too chummy with you." Hank pouted.

"He's married and is old enough to be my dad."

"Don't care. I saw the way he looked at you."

"Oh, for fuck's sake, is this what I have to look forward to? A jealous Hank Parker is an annoying Hank Parker."

"Get used to it. You're stuck with me for life."

"Not unless the zombies are unleashed."

"Huh," Lucas remarked. "You're right Miranda Panda they are fun to watch."

"Do not call me that!"

"What do you mean, Miranda Panda?" Lucas' face broke into amusement.

"I'll kill you."

"I'd like to see you try."

"That's it." Miranda turned to Olive, before kissing her lightly on the cheek. "I'll see you in the car. I can't be around this dickwad another second." Miranda started walking out of the room, with Lucas following right behind her. "Oh, the way you sway those hips." He groaned. "Miranda Panda, I'd follow you anywhere."

Once they were out of the room Olive turned to Hank, her brow raised.

"I don't know," he said. "We're just gonna have to sit back and watch."

"I'll bring the popcorn."

"Deal." Hank stood before retrieving the wheelchair. "Let's get you home."

Home.

Olive smiled as she stared at him. Home, that is precisely where she wanted to go. Home with Hank. "I love you."

Hank's whole face lit. "I love you too, Olive." He placed the wheelchair in front of her before gently grabbing her at the waist and placing her in the chair, with zero effort on his part.

"No manhandling," Olive joked which cause Hank to shake his head with a smile.

"Sure thing, Olive Oil. No manhandling." Hank pushed the chair out of the room. "Now, let's go home. I know Dog has a few words she'd like to discuss with you."

CHAPTER TWENTY-ONE

"STOP LOOKING AT ME LIKE THAT," Olive growled as she glared at Dog.

It had been a total of seven weeks. Seven freaking weeks since she had been released from the hospital. And, at this point, she was confident she was going to either pull her hair out or murder Hank in his sleep.

Either would suffice right now.

Dog looked Olive directly in the eyes before she hissed.

"Do not speak to me in that tone of voice, young lady," Olive growled. "I'm doing this for a reason."

Dog jumped onto the bed in Olive's room, which had also become Hank's room since coming home from the hospital. The creature then walked over to the see-through lingerie Olive was about to put on and plopped down onto it.

"You have got to be kidding me. Why are you being such a bully?" Olive tried to push Dog off the material only to be rewarded with a smack from her paw.

She pulled back her hand and made sure there weren't any lacerations. Thankfully, for her and Dog's sake, there weren't. Olive threw her head back before pleading with the ceiling.

Please give me the strength to not kill this cat. Or, if you're being super generous, can you distract her long enough I can lock her in the bathroom. Sure, I know I'll be signing my own death warrant, but I have needs.

Olive decided on changing tactics. "Did you know you're such a pretty kitty? So strong, and forceful. Right now, I'm trying to seduce your daddy tonight. If you let me have this I promise tuna dinners for the rest of your life."

Dog wasn't impressed. Instead, she yawned showing her teeth.

Olive glared at the ceiling. "Why, universe, freaking why?" She threw her body onto the bed, letting her crutches fall next to her. "Forget it," she huffed.

It's not like Hank would have wanted her anyway.

Sure, he was the loving and caring boyfriend she knew he would be since coming home from the hospital. He always made sure she had everything she needed. He was always there with her medicines, food, water, an extra pillow. You name it, he did it.

Hell, that first week he carried her everywhere. He waited on her hand and freaking foot. And she was grateful for him. She really was. He was absolutely the perfect boyfriend.

Except for one thing.

Olive threw her arm over her eyes.

No matter how many times she hinted at it, or tried to get things going, Hank refused to touch her.

Zero. Zip. Nada. Nothing.

She was about to lose her ever-loving mind.

Every shower she took, he was right there with her. He was meticulous at washing every inch of her body, but he refused to linger in any one spot.

She'd rub up against him, only for Hank to adjust to make sure she had more room.

He was driving her crazy.

It was almost as if she was this delicate piece of glass and he was being extra careful not to break her.

Give me a fucking break! She huffed into the room.

Other than some sore spots and her leg still being in a cast, she was fine for some extracurricular activities.

And it was about damn time.

Tonight was going to be the night she proved that to him.

Too bad stupid Dog had other plans.

Ever since Olive arrived home, Dog had taken it upon herself to be her "guard dog" in every sense of the word.

Dog refused to leave her side. When Hank started helping Olive learn how to use the crutches, Dog was there underfoot. At first, Olive was sure the creature was trying to trip her, but Olive soon realized Dog was actually escorting her.

Dog would walk a few feet ahead of Olive, then circle back and make sure there was nothing in the way that Olive would trip over.

Then there were times Olive wanted to hobble into the kitchen. If Hank weren't around Dog would yell at the top of her lungs, until she got his attention or she'd plop herself into Olive's lap refusing to move.

When Dog wanted you to stay put, you stayed put. No amount of pushing or shoving would get her to move.

Dog would somehow will her body to weigh an extra fifty pounds. And, that was exactly what Dog had decided on doing right now.

Apparently, Dog deemed sexy times as too risky and she was going to stop at nothing to cock block Olive.

"Between you and Hank, I'm never gonna get any," Olive groaned in frustration. With her good leg, she kicked one of her crutches causing it to fall to the floor making a loud crash.

One, two, three...

Hank burst through the bedroom door. "What happened, are you okay?" He ran to her side before picking up the crutch that fell.

"Nothing happened." Olive opened her eyes to see Hank staring down at her, one of the crutches in his right hand.

"Why did I hear a crash?"

"I don't know, maybe because that stupid thing fell over. It isn't rocket science."

Hank placed the crutch on the side of the bed before turning his attention back on her. "Are you hungry?"

Am I hungry? Olive stared at him wide-eyed.

Hank motioned to her body. "Why are you only wearing panties? Do you need me to help you get dressed?"

Was he serious right now? Wonderful. This is what her life had come to. "Just go."

"I'm not going anywhere." Hank took a step closer to the bed. "What's going on? Is Dog bothering you?" Hank focused his gaze on the cat, glaring at her. "Do I need to put her in timeout?"

She'd like to see him try.

"Between you and Dog I give up. Just go back to converting your room to an office," she mumbled before she threw her arm over her eyes once more.

"Are you in pain?"

That was it. She'd had enough. Olive threw her arm off of her face before she pushed herself into the seated position. "Yes, I'm in pain," she growled.

"What's hurting you? You said you were feeling good this morning. Did something happen?"

"Not that kind of pain."

Olive noticed her eyes were level with Hank's groin, and that seemed only to piss her off more. She gathered all her strength and pushed at his stomach as hard as she could causing Hank to trip backward.

"What the hell was that for?"

What the fuck?

Hank watched as Olive fell back onto the bed in a huff. He couldn't help that his eyes honed in on her naked breasts bouncing. His mouth watered at the sight. It took everything inside of him not to groan.

He selfishly let his eyes scan her body. All she wore was a pair of tiny dark green lace panties that failed to cover anything.

Give me strength. Please, fuckin' hell, give me strength.

Hank dug his fingernails into the palms of his hands. Seeing her body right now had him seconds from losing all control. The only thing keeping himself in check was the way Olive was acting.

Doing what he'd been doing since Olive came home from the hospital, he pushed away his desire for her and focused on getting her whatever she needed to feel better. "What do you need?"

"I'm tired," Olive sighed. "I'm gonna take a nap."

Hank's brows shot up. Did she think he was dumb?

Hank walked to the bed before he pushed Dog down. That's when he saw the dark green lace the cat had been sitting on top of. The same lace that matched Olive's panties.

"Olive?" He held up the material getting his first good look at it.

Lord have mercy!

Was she trying to kill him? Or, was she finally going to get him back for all the years he teased her with *this*?

When Olive saw him holding up the garment she snatched it from his grasp. "Not for you!"

Hank's eyes darkened. "It looks like it's for me."

He felt his dick twitch. He'd promised himself he'd wait until Olive was fully healed before he let himself lose control, but just the image of Olive dressed in this had every muscle in his body tensing.

"Then if it looks like it's for you, why don't you put it on? I'm sure the color would complement your eyes."

Oh, now this was the Olive he missed. The feisty Olive that made his whole world come alive.

And, if that Olive wanted to come out and play, he was damn well going to give it to her.

"One."

Olive shot up. "What?"

Hank ignored her as he climbed over to her. He threw his right leg over her hip pinning her down. "Two."

Olive's breath hitched as her eyes filled with lust.

Oh, she definitely wanted to play. *Thank God.* He didn't know how much longer he'd be able to handle cold showers.

"Hank Parker, I swear to everything I will murder you," she growled.

Her words said one thing, but the grinding of her hips against his groin said another.

In one fast move, Hank pinned her hands above her head which caused her breasts to bounce once again. "I know what you're doing," he remarked before he bent taking one of her nipples into his mouth.

Her taste exploded over his senses.

It was like coming home.

"I'm not doing anything!" Olive arched into his mouth, but he wasn't going to let her win. At least not yet.

He pulled his mouth away from her. At her growl of frustration, he smirked. "Oh, my poor Olive Oil, why such the long face?"

Olive narrowed her eyes at him as her lips thinned. "Are you making fun of me?"

"Now, would I ever do that?" he asked before bending once more to swipe his tongue across her peak.

"Yes, you would," she gasped.

When he pulled away again he felt her whole body start to shake. "I wonder what's got you so tense?" Hank readjusted himself so he had both of her arms pinned with only one of his hands.

Hank then proceeded to lightly trace her skin with his fingertips.

Then out of nowhere, he leaped off the bed. "I'll be right back with some food for you. You seem *'hangry'*."

Hank only made it one step before Olive jumped off the bed balancing on her good leg and tackled him.

Thank God he saw it coming or he wouldn't have been able to use his body as a cushion as they fell to the floor.

"You bastard!"

"That's not a nice thing to say," he growled before letting his hands skim up her body to cup her breasts.

"Neither is teasing me. And that's all you've been doing for weeks." She glared at him. "I have needs and you refuse to see to them. You can't give me access to all this..." She swept her hand down his body. "And then just take it away."

Thank fuck!

"I didn't take it away."

"Yes, you did. You gave me all the goods then you took them away and hid them in a box. Give me back my box!"

Hank threw Olive up into his arms as he pulled both of them off the floor. He then tossed her onto the bed. "Olive Quinn, or should I say Quinn Sparks, I never took myself away from you. In fact, it's nearly killed me being so close to you every second and *not* being able to touch you 'cause you were healing." He climbed up the bed to be directly over her. "Tell me, what would one of your characters have done in your books? Would they have pouted and tried to pick fights or would they have come to their man and tell them what they needed? If you wanted me, all you had to do was ask."

"I tried!" she pleaded. "I ordered that stupid nightie and your beast cat refused to let me seduce you."

Hank's brow rose while Olive continued. "I've been dropping hints like crazy. When we're in the shower, sitting together, or when we're in bed and I rub against you. But you ignored me. You ignored every attempt I have tried. Then I got the bright idea I could seduce you with some lace. I know how you love lace. I was going to put it on, and call you into the room, but your stupid cat cock blocked me. I want sex and I want it now!"

Hank burst out laughing.

Why is she so perfect?

When he saw her gaze drop away from him and the tears form in her eyes he realized his mistake.

"Are you laughing at me?"

He quickly leaned over her body kissing her cheeks. "No baby, I'm not laughing at you."

She looked at him skeptically.

"I'm laughing at all the effort you put into this. You didn't have to. Olive, I've been dying to sink myself into your body again. Once you've had perfection, your hand just won't do. All you had to do was tell me, baby. I'd gladly let you take a ride on me. I was only being cautious. I didn't want to accidentally cause you any more pain."

"The only pain I have right now is not being with you," she cried.

"You sure your leg doesn't hurt?" he joked which caused her to growl. "Kidding." Hank righted himself before pulling his shirt over his head. "I've rubbed myself raw over the past few weeks not being able to touch you."

"Rub me. Not you."

"Oh, baby, I plan on it." You didn't have to tell him twice,

Hank expertly lowered himself between her legs. He carefully moved her leg that was still in the cast so he wouldn't bump into it, before he positioned his face more freely at her core.

Shit, it had been too long.

Olive started rocking her hips as Hank pushed her panties to the side.

"You look good enough to eat," he growled. "And I am one starving man." He took one long lick of her pussy relishing in her taste.

"Yes, please," she begged.

Hank moved his gaze from her core to her face. Fuck she was so beautiful.

And all his.

He didn't know what he would have done if she hadn't have made it.

"I love you," he said, looking into her eyes.

"I love you, too. Now less talking more fucking."

He shook his head. If his girl wanted to be fucked, then he was going to fuck her.

He jumped off the bed, before discarding his pants.

"No come back!" she cried.

"Oh, I'm coming, and so are you." After disrobing he crawled back onto the bed before he wrapped his hand around Olive's panties. With the snap of his wrist, they ripped from her body.

"Hey! Those were expensive!"

"Don't care." He shrugged before opening her legs with his knees. He moved his hips forward and positioned himself at her entrance. "You want this?"

"You know I do." She glared. "Right now, it's been too long since I've had you inside of me and if you make me wait a second more, I am going to poison your coffee and pretend the cat did it. Remind me of what I've been missing and give me a reason to never look anywhere else."

"Oh, you are gonna get it." Hank grabbed onto her hips before thrusting.

Her walls instantly clamping around him sent a wave of pleasure through his body.

Fuck, how was it possible she feels this good? He slowly pulled out before pushing back inside with more force.

"Yes! More! Give it to me, Hank. Give me something to write about."

She wanted something to write about? Well, he was going to give it to her.

He fought himself to hold back some. He knew he needed to be gentle with her body, but there was something that made him snap when it came to Olive.

He wasn't ashamed of that.

Not wanting to chance hurting her, Hank grabbed her waist flipping them, so she could ride him. "You won't get hurt this way," he explained as Olive flailed around trying to reposition herself.

"You could have warned me."

"I did, just now." Hank placed his hands on her hips helping guide her movements. "Ride me, Olive. Fucking ride me like I'm your man."

"You are my man," she moaned as she started to move her hips along with his.

"Don't you ever fucking forget it."

Hank thrust his hips upwards pushing himself deeper inside of Olive. He then moved his right hand down to her clit, pinching it. "I can't last baby, not after not having you," he panted as he felt his body tense. "I need you to come for me, Olive. I'll make it better next time, but right now I need you to come with me."

Hank felt Olive's body start to shake as her movements became more erratic.

"More," she cried.

He reached his hand to her breasts pinching her nipple. That's when she exploded.

He only needed to push in her one more time before his whole body stilled as he emptied himself deep inside of her.

Home.

He was home.

They both fell back onto the bed, Olive resting her body on his as they both tried to catch their breath.

"That's all I asked for, was that so hard?" Olive mumbled into his chest.

Hank couldn't help his smirk before he spanked her ass. "One."

CHAPTER TWENTY-TWO

Six Months Later

HANK PACED INSIDE the living room as his nerves started to get the better of him. He'd sent Olive a text about twenty minutes ago letting her know he had a surprise for her, and if she wanted it she needed to meet him at the address he'd given her.

Now, as the time ticked by he wondered if he'd done the right thing. Sure, he wanted to take the next step. Hell, he wanted to take the next step months ago, but when it came to Olive, he wanted to make sure everything was perfect.

Hank glanced around the room one more time before he assessed that everything seemed to be in order, or as much in order as they were going to get.

Around four months ago, he'd been on shift when he drove past a Victorian style house that had gone up for sale.

Normally, such things wouldn't have caught his attention, but there was something about this house that called to him.

Maybe it was the wrap around porch, or maybe it was its sea blue color that reminded him of Olive's eyes. Maybe, it was all the uniqueness in the house with its genuine quirks and homey feel? He wasn't quite sure, but regardless, he knew he was staring at the home he wanted to raise his family in.

A family he wanted with no one other than Olive.

Hank's face lit into a gorgeous smile.

Olive and his relationship had only gotten better since declaring their love for one another, in his opinion. Well, they still had their arguments, and he still swore she picked fights on purpose for make-up sex, but they were going strong. And it was about time they took the next step.

After Olive's cast was removed, she looked as good as new. You wouldn't have been able to tell she was ever in a car crash that threatened to take her from him other than some scars. Scars that he now deemed her survival wounds. And they were fucking beautiful, and if anyone thought differently, he would gladly rearrange their face.

Olive was the reason Hank woke up in the mornings, and he didn't care who knew it.

That's why when he saw their perfect house for sale, he had to have it.

He knew beyond a reasonable doubt, this was the house him and Olive would raise their family in.

Hank's chest puffed as he took another glance around the room.

He'd spent the last four months completely renovating the house to the exact way he knew Olive would love it. He was damn thankful that his family and buddies at the station agreed to help him in the process. Without them, he was sure it would have been another four or five months to accomplish what he wanted.

Everything had worked out perfectly. Since Olive was back to writing full time, it gave Hank the opportunity to "leave her to her writing" and work on the house. In actuality, he was almost positive Olive hadn't registered he was gone longer than his shifts entailed.

Plus, his genius self came up with the best incentive for Olive to keep her head in her writing and not question why he wasn't around as much.

He'd be lying if he said it didn't benefit both of them.

Each day, Olive would set a word count. If she met that word count by the time he'd gotten home from his shift, he'd go down on her for five minutes straight. Then for every thousand she went over her word count, he'd add on another minute.

Her daily word count goals were around three thousand, but she'd always end up with ten to twelve thousand, it was a win-win if you asked him.

Especially, for the days she didn't complete her word count. For those rare occurrences she didn't make her count, she'd go down on him for the same time he would have gone down on her.

Either way, it always ended in the exact place they both wanted to be, with him deep inside of her.

Plus, this helped her crank out another book.

Who knew the incentive of eating out her pussy would make Olive write like her ass was on fire?

You wouldn't hear any complaints from him though. Every night on his way home, he'd have a hard dick in his pants and a smile on his face.

Fuck yeah, his life was awesome.

As Hank reveled in how perfect his relationship with Olive was, he heard Dog make her way into the room.

He had to fight back his grin as she plopped in front of him, glaring at him.

"Be a good sport, Dog. It's only until mom gets here." Hank watched as Dog scratched at her sweater trying to rip it off her body. On one hand he didn't blame her, who would want to wear that ridiculous getup? But on the other, she just needed to suck it up for twenty minutes.

We all did things we didn't like for the people we love. Hence the constant Bigfoot marathons he watched on tv.

"Leave it." Hank rolled his eyes. "Let Olive have this moment, okay? I promise as soon as she sees you, we will take it off."

Dog hissed in his direction.

He winced. *Maybe I should have left her in the apartment?* When Dog opened her mouth again, she broadcasted her sharp teeth. *Was this how Olive felt?*

Now he understood why Olive was always so adamant about Dog trying to make a meal out of her when he first moved into her apartment. He decided he didn't want to anger the beast any more than he had. He made the move to remove the sweater from Dog when he heard Olive's car pull into the driveway.

He froze.

"Sorry, girl. It's showtime."

Olive huffed as she pulled into the driveway of the address Hank sent her. She couldn't help but be a little miffed he hadn't given her any information other than "I need you to come to this address".

For all she knew, someone could have stolen his phone and this was a setup. What if it was the government finally going after her after all her years of spouting the existence of Bigfoot and Aliens?

This could be her end.

Or worse.

What if this was a party he wanted her to attend.

That's probably exactly what this was. Knowing Hank this was his attempt to get her to go outside but do it in a sneaky way as to not freak her out.

Well, he was wrong.

This did freak her out.

She needed to be warned at least three days in advance if she was to have other human interaction. It was a common courtesy.

Plus, if Olive were being honest, she wasn't fully comfortable driving on her own yet. No one could blame her. Although, most of her nightmares had disappeared, she still had a tiny fear of getting behind the wheel.

Once Olive had gotten a clean bill of health from the doctor, Hank and Miranda forced her to get a brand new car.

A safe car.

This one had brakes that worked wonderfully, and she knew that. However, she still wasn't comfortable driving without someone in the passenger seat.

That whole stronger in numbers thing really spoke to her.

Hank knew that.

She narrowed her eyes. After whatever this *was* ended, she was going to give Hank an earful and then make him sleep on the couch.

Olive shut off the car and hopped out into the driveway. That's when she got her first good look at the house.

She stopped dead in her tracks.

The house was absolutely breathtaking.

Olive had never seen anything so beautiful in her life. Quickly she pulled out her phone and started snapping pictures. "This is one hundred percent going into my next book." Olive continued to take pictures until she realized what a creeper she was being. She sighed before she placed her phone in her back pocket.

Might as well get this over with.

Cautiously, she walked to the front door before ringing the bell.

Please let this be easy. Please let this be easy.

"The door's open!"

"Hank is that you?" she asked as she reached for the handle.

"Yeah, come in, baby."

Olive pushed open the door only to freeze in her tracks.

There in front of her was a room filled to the brim with holiday decorations. There was garland hung from the fireplace and all around the banisters. There were candles and lights everywhere the eye could see.

It was like Christmas threw up.

And she loved every single second of it.

As Olive tried to control her rampant heartbeat her mind started to register everything she was seeing.

That's when Hank came into view.

He stood in front of one of the largest Christmas trees Olive had ever seen.

She stood there in awe as she took in all of his glory. He wore dark blue jeans and a maroon long sleeve shirt, that made him look like a model come to life. That wasn't the best part though. No, Hank Parker also wore a Santa hat.

"What's going on?" she asked as she took a step closer to him while she cocked her head to the side.

That's when out of the corner of her eye she saw Dog. "Oh my word, why is Dog wearing an ugly Christmas sweater, and how in the hell did you get it on her and not end up in the emergency room?" Olive shot her head from Dog to Hank and then back again. "Wait, why is Dog even here? I thought she was at home. How did I miss you taking her out of the apartment? No, wait, why are you wearing a Santa hat?" Olive threw her hands in the air. "I have so many questions!" Olive watched as Dog tried to fight with the sweater before flopping onto the floor giving up, but not before glaring at Hank.

Olive had to bite her cheek not to laugh at the sight before her.

"I said give it twenty minutes, Dog," Hank growled. "That's all I asked. Why do you have to be so goddamn stubborn?"

Olive snapped her gaze back to Hank, as she did her best not to burst out in laughter. "Hank?"

"Dog's just being dramatic," he assured Olive. "She'll probably murder me in my sleep tonight, but it'll be worth it."

Olive quirked her brow at him. "What?"

Hank cleared his throat before taking a step closer to Olive. He then opened his arms. "Welcome home, baby."

"Home?"

Olive looked around the room, her eyes wide as she took everything in as the word home rang throughout her head.

"When I came across this house for sale I knew it was the one for us," Hank spoke softly. "I wanted to surprise you."

"This is your home?" she asked completely dumbfounded.

He bought a house? Like as in a place you live?

"Our home," he corrected. "I bought this place and fixed it up for us. It has a master bedroom on the second floor, and three additional bedrooms for when we have children." He winked at her. "If you think the living room is full of Christmas you should see your office I set up off the kitchen."

Olive tried to make sense of everything Hank was telling her, but she was coming up short.

To her utter surprise, Hank lowered himself to his knee. "I knew this house was the one we would raise our children in. I have no doubt in my mind about that. I also know you aren't the biggest fan of change, so I figured I would take all the stress and unknown out of the equation and place your mind at ease by just doing it." He motioned to the room around him. "The Christmas tree in our bedroom reminds you you're free and I love that about you. While you're in our home I want you to always remember you are free. We'll keep the decorations up all year long if that's what makes you happy. If not, there is a Christmas tree in the master bedroom that will stay up all year. We can binge watch zombie movies in the comfort of our own winter wonderland." Hank pulled out a small box from his jeans. "All you have to do is say yes and we can start our conspiracy filled, holiday infused, lives together."

Tears formed in Olive's eyes as she watched the man she loved give her everything she'd ever dreamed she wanted. Olive had always wanted a happy ending like she wrote about in her stories, but this was better.

This was real life.

A lopsided grin formed on Olive's face. "What exactly am I saying yes to?"

Hank's brows shot to the ceiling before a wide smile spread across his face. "One."

Oh, for the love of...

Olive rolled her eyes before she ran toward Hank jumping into his arms.

When they both fell back onto the floor Olive started to smother Hank in kisses. "I'm not saying yes until you ask me properly," she teased as she kissed along his jawline.

"Fine, you pain in my ass." Hank rolled Olive under him. "Would you put me out of my misery and marry me?"

Olive's heart was seconds from exploding. "Now, was that so hard? All you had to do was ask."

"Is that a yes?"

"Of course, it's a yes!" Olive pushed Hank's shoulders making him fall onto his ass. That's when Olive jumped to her feet running back to the front room toward the stairs.

"Where the hell do you think you're going?" Hank growled, as he started to chase after her.

"I've got some exploring to do." Olive raced up the stairs. "Someone decided to buy the house I'm going to live in for the rest of my life without consulting me first. I need to make sure it's up to my standards," she teased.

"Two."

Olive stopped once she made it halfway up the stairs before she pivoted back to face Hank. "You've got to catch me first."

Olive took off up the stairs leaving Hank at the bottom a broad smile going across his face.

"Oh, I plan on it." He took off in a full sprint after her as he yelled out, "Three!"

Thank you for reading Teased by Fire. I hope you enjoyed it. Do you want to know if Lord Waffles will rule the world? Did you enjoy the very opinionated Corgi, his accident prone mom, Holly and her Adonis veterinarian husband, Ben?

If so check out their story in Stumbling Into Him.

Look for a sneak peek on the next page.

Did you enjoy Lucas and Miranda?

They will be getting their own standalone book too. Keep an eye out for more information on their story.

STUMBLING INTO HIM SNEAK PEEK

Chapter One

"WATCH OUT!"

Holly Flanagan heard a commotion coming from the other side of the park.

Ignoring the shouting, she bent over focusing on picking up her Corgi, Waffles', most recent deposit. With Holly's track record, though, she should have known anyone yelling "watch out," "take cover," or "that's about to fall" was directed at her. Even after years of being the spokesperson for unlucky, klutzy, and clumsy she still disregarded the shouting as she carried on with her dog parent duties.

Before she could register what happened, she was knocked onto her back with a pain radiating from her mouth and nose.

"At least the sky is pretty today," Holly mumbled as she tried to get her bearings. She reached for her mouth as she felt the pain start to spread.

"Ma'am, are you okay?"

Holly closed her eyes as she thought about it.

Was she okay? She'd just been hit with something. She was pretty sure some part of her face, she didn't know which part, but she was sure something was bleeding. Waffles barked uncontrollably, and her head hurt.

So, was she okay?

Holly let out a heavy sigh.

Yeah, she was fine. This was just another day in her life for her. And so far, if being hit by an unknown projectile to the face was the worst thing that happened to her, she'd considered it a good day.

Deciding to face the music she opened her eyes.

Holy shit!

Above her, only a mere few inches from her face was by far the most handsome man she had ever laid eyes on.

He had dark brown hair and deep blue eyes that were richer than the ocean. His jaw was chiseled, with a light dusting of scruff, in the alpha male, I'm in charge here kind of way.

Wonderful. Okay, let's add embarrassing yourself in front of a Greek God to your list of attributes for the day. Hey, it can only get better from here, right?

When she realized she'd been staring at him for what could have been considered too long, she quickly jerked her head forward trying to right herself. Unfortunately for her, though, she slammed her head right into the Greek God's forehead.

Freaking wonderful.

Not only was her mouth hurting, her head now pounded.

Absolutely freaking wonderful!

"Shit," she heard the Greek God say as the wave of pain coursed through her body.

Taking the chance, she opened her eyes again only to see her Adonis holding his head. *Great.* And to make matters worse, Waffles started barking directly at her before looking at his recent deposit still on the ground then back at her.

"For the love of all things, dog. I was trying to pick it

up," she growled, before taking her hand away from her mouth to deal with his majesty, *Lord* Waffles. However, the second her hand came into view she saw the blood and screamed.

"Oh shit. Lady, you're bleeding," the Adonis said, putting his hand under her chin moving it from side to side as he examined her face.

"What happened?" Panic ran through her. *Did I break my nose? Am I unconscious? Am I dying?*

The Adonis tilted her chin back to get a better look. "I was tossing the Frisbee with Ripley, and somehow it veered off course. I tried to warn you with the 'watch out.'"

Typical. Holly groaned. *Hot guy throws Frisbee. Said Frisbee hits me in the face. Hot guy then insinuates it's my fault for not getting out of the way fast enough. I mean, I know I'm generally invisible to men like him, but, damn. You'd think these extra wide hips would make me more visible.* She glared at the Frisbee sitting next to her.

Ignoring the object, she moved her eyes back to the Adonis.

"I can't tell if it's a busted lip or worse." He tilted her head further back like she was a child.

Holly ripped her face from his hand. She'd be able to tell if it was just a busted lip. She'd had too many to count in her life, from falling down, objects to the face, and even falling up the stairs. She reached into her pocket and pulled out the napkin she had stuffed in there from her soft pretzel. She blew off some stray salt and started feverishly wiping at her mouth.

"Let me see," he demanded, before taking one of the napkins from her hand. He then started dabbing at her lips.

She froze.

Well, Holly. This is the most action you've had in months. And, if some hot guy is all over you, you might as well enjoy it while it lasts.

Waffles crawled onto her lap demanding attention and started kissing the underside of her jaw.

Thanks, Waffles, for bringing the attention of my double chin to the Adonis. She rolled her eyes.

"Thanks for trying to help me clean up your mom," the Adonis remarked before quickly abandoning his job of cleaning the blood off her mouth to pat Waffles on the head.

"He's not trying to help you," Holly scoffed. "He's *trying* to remind me I still need to pick up his poop and then give him a treat."

"Shouldn't your mom be the one getting the treat if *she's* the one picking up your shit?" He cocked his head at her dog.

Waffles, ever the one to argue, looked at the man that now had a mischievous grin on his face, with the most judgmental side-eye he could muster.

No one came between him and his treats.

Ignoring Waffles' attempt at a threat, the Adonis once again pat the dog on the head before moving back to Holly's mouth dismissing him. "I think it's just a busted lip, but your front tooth..." He coughed as he sheepishly looked away.

"My front tooth?" Holly quickly ran her tongue along her front teeth. Shit, she felt a jagged piece. "Oh, crap." She quickly pulled her phone from her pocket and launched the front-facing camera.

As soon as she saw her face, she jerked back. Her hair was all over the place, her face red, there was still blood on her...

You've had better days, Holly. She took a deep breath before he hastily opened her mouth to see the damage.

"Oh no."

Staring back at her was a chipped front tooth along with a busted lip. *Wonderful. Thank you so much, Universe. Thank you, so very much.* She didn't know whether she wanted to laugh or cry. *Clumsy Holly, strikes again. Do you ever take a break?*

As her eyes flooded with tears a sudden cold nose hit her

arm distracting her. Realizing it wasn't Waffles she looked to her left and saw one of the most beautifully colored gray and black Australian Shepherds she'd ever seen.

"Aren't you a cutie?" she softly said. Thankfully, her love of animals overrode everything she was feeling.

"That's Ripley." The Greek God chuckled. "I'd thought you'd be more concerned about your mouth than a dog."

Ignoring him, she reached out to scratch Ripley's chin. "You're so pretty." Ripley must have agreed because she barked before kissing Holly's hand.

"Uhh, ma'am, I'm not a human doctor but I think we should pay more attention to your injuries instead of the dogs."

"Human doctor?" Her brows shot up. "As opposed to what, an alien doctor?"

"I haven't worked on any aliens that I know of, but I did neuter a cat named Alien once. Does that count?"

Her eyes widened at the realization. "Oh great, you've got a body of a Greek God, and now you're also a vet. Which of course means you love animals. *Freakin'* wonderful. You're like the most perfect guy, and here I am on the sidewalk with blood pouring out of me with a chipped tooth." She pushed Waffles off her lap and stood. "Please excuse me while I find a place to die of embarrassment."

A corner of the sexy man's mouth lifted. "You're funny."

"And you're hot. So, we've now successfully established which groups we belong to." Annoyed at herself more than anything she angrily started to stomp away from the Greek God.

"Hey, wait up!"

She spun around to glare at him. When Holly saw Waffles sitting at the foot of the Adonis looking up at him, her left eye started to twitch.

Of course, her dog would betray her. She wouldn't expect

anything less. "Waffles, come." She pulled on the leash slightly, but the dog wouldn't move. "Lord Waffles, get your butt over here."

The man cocked his brow. "Lord Waffles?"

"Yeah," she answered. "He thinks he's a freakin' king. Hence the "lord" and I love waffles. Do you got a problem with that, buster?"

The Adonis burst into laughter as he scratched Waffles on the back. To make matters worse, that betraying Corgi rolled over onto his back asking for belly rubs.

The Audacity! *That's it. No more treats for you!* She glared at her dog.

"Who's a good boy?" the Adonis cooed. "You've got a weird name, but you're the best boy aren't cha?"

Holly's eye started to twitch harder.

She stomped back toward her bastard of a dog and the Greek God when out of nowhere her foot hit an invisible rock causing her to trip. Within a split second, she ended up falling right into the arms of the bane of her existence at the moment.

"Whoa, are you okay?"

"I'm fine," she grumbled as she righted herself. *Go ahead and add this to the, "it can only happen to me" list.*

"I feel like you need to walk around with a warning sign or at least a crash helmet," he joked.

"Not the first time I've heard that." Quickly she bent down and retrieved Waffles. "If you'll excuse me. Not only do I really need to find a secluded place to die of embarrassment, I also need to call my dentist, or go to the walk-in. Maybe both." She turned on her heel and started power walking down the sidewalk.

As she passed the spot she'd tripped at, she examined the cement. Figures, there'd be absolutely nothing there. If there were a sporting category on tripping over invisible objects she'd win gold twice over.

"Hey!"

She kept walking, doing her best to hide her humiliation and ignore the Greek God.

Unfortunately, that was short-lived. "Hey, I want to make sure you really are okay," he said, as he caught up to her in two point three seconds.

Stupid short legs! "I'm fine."

"Your lip's still bleeding."

She glared at him. "Wonderful."

"Hey..." He reached for her arm stopping her escape.

"What?"

"Let me help you. My practice is only a block from here. I've got all the supplies to clean up your lip. I can also get a better look at your tooth."

"You're a vet." Her eyes started to twitch again. *Could today get any worse?*

"I am pretty sure if I can surgically remove nuts from an animal I can look at your busted lip." He shrugged before smirking at her.

A laugh escaped her lips. He did have a point after-all. "Thank you for the offer...." she trailed off.

"Ben. The name's Ben Richman." He held out his hand to her.

"Thanks for the offer Dr. Richman, but there is a walk-in clinic not far from where I live."

"Call me Ben. And please let me do this. It'll help me sleep at night knowing the woman I maimed with a Frisbee is some- what okay." She watched as his eyes pleaded with her. Even Waffles, the jerk, who was still in her arms looked up at her and whined. "Oh, for the love of... fine. Lead the way, Ben."

"Perfect." Ben's mouth curved into a smile. "Follow me."

When he whistled Ripley sat instantly by his side. He quickly bent down and fastened her leash before walking toward the street.

Holly looked at Waffles who was clearly enjoying being carried. "Guess you get an extra trip to the vet."

She couldn't help but burst out laughing when Waffles closed his mouth and glared at her.

Find out what happens next in Stumbling Into Him.

ALSO BY MOLLY O'HARE

Hollywood Hopeful Series

Hollywood Dreams

Risking It All (Danny and Lexi's Story) – *Coming soon*

Stumbling Through Life

Stumbling Into Him

Stumbling Into Forever

Teased Series

Teased by Fire -*This book*

Lucas & Miranda's story- *coming soon*

Standalone

Nothing But a Dare

Learning Curves

Stay up to date on New Releases

Sign up for my newsletter by clicking the link or going to my
website: MollyOHareauthor.com

Check out the Fun Facts on the next page.

ABOUT THE AUTHOR

Much like any author out there, sleeping does not come easily to me. It turns out I have the worst insomnia of anyone I have ever met. Since I was a little girl, to help myself fall asleep, I would recite stories. Each night I would pick up where the story left off previously until the tale was complete. One morning, after I finished a particularly fun story, I decided I wanted to start sharing them with others. A few months later, here I am, sharing my lack of sleep with all of you. Who says the stories in our heads can't be fun for others?

I think I will bestow upon you some fun facts about me.

Fun Facts for Teased by Fire:

I have two cats named after the Muppets, Beaker and Bunsen Honeydew.

I hiked a mountain in Colorado this summer... and didn't die.

I poked myself in the eye this morning, because I forgot I was wearing my contacts instead of my glasses.

I don't eat any type of ground beef. The texture is really weird to me... No hamburgers for this girl!

Corgi butts still drive me nuts.

Stay Connected

facebook.com/MollyOHareAuthor

instagram.com/mollyohareauthor

goodreads.com/MollyOHare

bookbub.com/profile/molly-o-hare

Made in the USA
Coppell, TX
02 June 2021

56679969R00125